RUSSIAN STORIES

RUSSIAN STORIES

Francesc Serés

**Translated from the Russian by
Anastasia Maximova**

**Translated from the Catalan by
Peter Bush**

MACLEHOSE PRESS
QUERCUS · LONDON

First published in the Catalan language as *Contes russos*
by Quaderns Crema, S.A.U., Barcelona, in 2009
First published in Great Britain in 2013 by

MacLehose Press
an imprint of Quercus
55 Baker Street
7th Floor, South Block
London W1U 8EW

The translation of this work was supported by a grant from the Institut Ramon Llull

LLLL institut
ramon llull
Catalan Language and Culture

ISBN (HB) 978 0 85705 158 5
ISBN (TPB) 978 0 85705 159 2
ISBN (Ebook) 978 0 85705 160 8

10 9 8 7 6 5 4 3 2

Designed and typeset in Quadraat by Libanus Press
Printed and bound in Great Britain by Clays Ltd, St Ives plc

RUSSIAN STORIES

CONTENTS

JOSSEF BERGCHENKO

My great-grandmother always told anyone prepared to listen to her that they should make portraits of Stalin and Lenin like icons, and that Marx was really a member of the church, with that patriarch's beard of his, and would be venerated by everyone the day he dressed like a saint and was photographed inside a church.

NIKITA REVUNOV
A Groundswell of Groans

Life unleashes
earthquakes and eruptions,
hurricanes and floods
on my life.
Long stretches
of peace and quiet,
in deserts that freeze or burn,
and nights on stormy seas.
I know I am nothing,
am nobody,
but all there is what I am,
my all
is my life.

A.K. VOINITSKY
The Trapeze and the Net

"Quiet, quiet," said Grandad Prokofi, "quiet, quiet!" while he enthusiastically beat all the children who said they were his grandchildren with a stick

ANNA ANDREYEVA
Stories from Remote Hamlets

PREFACE

ANASTASIA MAXIMOVA

My family lived in the industrial area where my father worked. My world was school there, doctors there, school trips in buses there and games played in the sports halls there. The foundry chimneys and the grey clouds they spewed out dominated the whole district and were the centre of my world.

An esplanade in front of the blast furnaces was made from ten-centimetre-thick blocks of steel. The gantries operated by the workers emptied all manner of scrap metal onto the esplanade: they flattened cars, gutted tanks and armaments, sliced through silos and trucks, twisted rails and multiple items from diverse, unknown sources. They worked non-stop, mixed scrap with iron ore that piled up into what I thought looked like huge mountains. Hammers and crushers broke and smashed everything, the magnets hoisted the pieces and dropped them until the scraps were small enough for the gantries to load and then empty them into the furnaces.

The scrap metal reached the foundry in trucks pulled by the train that came from the city on the western track. Sometimes, the train transported another train, trucks, engine and all, that the cranes hoisted as high as possible with their magnets. Then they switched off the current and the items fell on the esplanade, dropped without a second glance. It was a sorry sight to see an old train appear on the back of a young one: we thought we could look into their eyes. Our only consolation was the thought they would extract metal from them to make new, more handsome specimens.

On the southeast track they unloaded mineral that still had to be melted and refined. The trucks were only a third full, Father said they had to be careful: if a convoy was overloaded, the weight might buckle the rails and derail the train. The trucks tipped their contents into a hopper that emptied them onto a conveyor belt. The belt lifted the mineral up and dropped it on the ground until it made a perfect cone that other conveyor belts transported to the furnaces.

The whole district was astounded the day statues, even some quite colossal figures, began rolling in. Political leaders were eradicating them from towns and cities of the Union. It was the 1990s, I had grown up and knew that those statues didn't simply represent what we were taught at school and I had also discovered there was more to the world than our district.

Stalins were the first to arrive, for some reason, and Lenins came months later. There were also some Marxes, but very few. Stalins arrived on special platforms, roped down on their side or sometimes they had been broken up, legs in one truck, head and body in another, sometimes in quite hilarious postures. As soon as Stalin was untied, the magnets lifted him up and dropped him onto the steel floor. Even when they were entangled in the folds of the overcoats the statues usually wore, the bodies and legs soon broke up after being dropped for a second or third time. However, the heads were often massive and solid and bounced. Some had been reinforced inside with various incredibly tough alloys. If they were small enough to enter the mouths of the furnaces, it was a simple process and the bodies slid inside as if it were a crematorium oven. But if they were too big, there was no way they could crack those heads open. They tried to slice or hack off part of the hair, the nose, the most prominent parts of the cheeks and cheekbones, but the saws bent and the enormously solid nostrils blunted their serrated edges. The only solution they found was to drill holes, fill them with an explosive charge, bury the heads underground and blow them up.

In the end it was too much work and they decided to let them be. Stalin's heads, disfigured by all the bangs and cuts they had received, were piled in a corner, from where they scrutinised the foundry cycle as it resumed time and again, the red hot iron gradually turning grey and black. The stories in this anthology speak of the gazes from those heads and the way *we* looked into their eyes, as we questioned them about the past that shaped them, and also about the more recent past that threw them into the air and broke them. But our questions and gazes went on to ask them much more about the years of indifference, the preceding years and, above all, the years to come. The stories also form part of the cycle that old stories and themes engage with, re-shaping and re-firing them yet again.

An old proverb says that a plant needs roots and flowers in order to live. And it is true, it needs light and darkness, air and earth, the past of the seed from which it came and the future of the seeds born from the fruit it will bear. When I read these stories in succession I felt the proverb was being made flesh. There are roots here, roots that are the stories and authors that time and the twists and turns of history have concealed from us, roots of the tasks the makers of the anthology have had to perform, and flowers, flowers in the form of stories their readers must bring to life.

I began to collect these flowers eight years ago, some from roadsides and places of transit, but others from distant fields, dangerous valleys and lofty peaks. There are canonical stories, anthologised elsewhere, like "The Forfeit" by Ola Yevgueniyeva, "Guilt" by Vera-Margarita Abanserev or "Elvis Presley Sings in Red Square" by Vitali Kroptkin. There are others, like "The Riders" by Jossef Bergchenko, published in a magazine in 1922 and not seen since. Or unfinished and unpublished stories, like "The War against the Voromians" by Aleksandr Volkov.

Salvaging these texts was a real challenge. This project could not have been brought to fruition without the support of the Department of Contemporary Literature in the University of Nizhny Novgorod. My thanks to all those who have collaborated – relatives, academics, collectors, archivists, curators, publishers and booksellers, all readers – without whom many of the texts in this anthology would have been completely forgotten.

Many years after their first readers held them in their hands, the stories by Jossef Bergchenko or Aleksandr Volkov and the characters that inspired them, having survived the era of Vitali Kroptkin, now join with the characters strolling through St Petersburg or Moscow in the stories by Ola Yevgueniyeva or Vera-Margarita Abanserev. The publication of this Catalan translation means all that work has borne fruit and that those roots that originated in Russia bear fruit today in Catalunya.

A FEW NOTES ON THE ANTHOLOGY

FRANCESC SERÉS

I.

I visited Minsk two years ago at the invitation of the Byelorussian critic Karl Batlovitch. The hotel he booked me into, one of the city's two or three prestige hotels, was near the centre.

The first morning I went down for breakfast I picked up a laminated sheet of paper, a photocopy of a photocopy of a photocopy – the menu. The menu in English was at the top and in the local language at the bottom. By each dish was a number that served to connect them in both languages. Apart from the omelette, the remaining options were only recognisable via English translation.

I ordered number 3, ham, but when it arrived, an omelette sat in the middle of my plate, an undercooked, greasy plain omelette. I told the waitress she had made a mistake, that the omelette must be for another table, but she rudely told me it wasn't, that it was mine. She seemed to be telling me to eat it, whether I liked it or not.

The following morning, that waitress was not on duty. I ordered ham, pointing to the ham on another table and they brought me ham. Juicy ham, juicy and off the bone. As on the previous day, I didn't risk the coffee.

On my third day, the waitress was back. I tried to avoid her radius of activity: if she went right, I went left; if she headed to the entrance,

I went towards the exit . . . A total waste of time, as soon as I sat down, she came and asked me what I wanted . . . and brought me another omelette. In protest, I cut it into thin slices and shaped them into a "NO" on my plate and left.

The fourth time I went into the dining room, I ordered ham for a fourth time; but before the waitress could return from the kitchen, I got up and spoke to the maître d', who theoretically knew a little English, and asked him why they brought me omelette when I had ordered ham.

He looked at the sheet, the menu, and said he didn't understand. I persisted. He told me to sit down, they'd bring me my ham; but when the waitress came, she brought me yet another omelette. I pursued the maître d', on my high horse, and dragged him by the arm to my table: an omelette.

The maître d' scratched the scruff of his neck, asked in the kitchen, asked the waitress and was none the wiser. That's to say, he looked at me as if I were an awkward customer, someone who orders an omelette and then complains when they bring it, saying he had ordered ham.

By the fifth day I was beginning to see this as a matter of honour, and was fortunate that a lady sitting on the next table, an air hostess, spoke both English and the local language. I asked her if she had had any problems or if they brought her what she ordered. Or if it was traditional to serve omelettes or if there was a five-year overproduction of eggs. The lady, who initially didn't understand what I was talking about and told the maître d' – already on his way, looking horrified – that there was nothing to worry about, then glanced at the menu and laughed. Someone had made a mistake copying out the translations and had put one dish down twice. As a result, 3 for ham became 3 for omelette and that meant the remaining dishes were out of order as well.

I checked the other menus that were photocopies of a photocopy . . .

I grabbed them all and went in pursuit of the maître d' who was begin-ning to look daggers at me. I told him it was all down to a mistake on the menu, that all the dishes in English were wrong. He said right, that was true, but as they had so few customers from abroad . . . I asked him if they would change them and he said they would, but the day after and subsequently the photocopies were the same, intact. I ordered number 4, which was a total mystery, but matched ham off the bone in the local language. And they brought it, looking equally sour, but they did bring it. After battling on so many mornings, I suddenly remembered some of the stories Anastasia had told me about and, in particular, their constant reference to exhaustion, resistance and hardness, as well as a sense of humour that is a form of resistance against injustice that reaches everywhere, even a tourist's breakfast.

2.

I met Anastasia Maximova at a writers' forum in Prague. I spoke about how difficult it was to describe the work of a turner and she talked about an author who had written several stories that were set in ball-bearing factories in Karkhov. The translation of that first story was followed by others we e-mailed to each other in Spanish. Of course, I didn't know Russian – and still don't – I recognise the alphabet and the script and can pronounce it, but I don't understand a word apart from those the Catalan language has incorporated in one way or another. Anastasia Maximova started sending me stories, excerpts from other writers that I mostly found to be excellent. The fact that our interests and tastes dovetail has been very helpful as we go about our corres-pondence, recovering these writers and making our final selection. Beyond her translating, Anastasia Maximova's contribution has been invaluable in terms of her choice of writers and stories, some of which – writers and stories – had been concealed by layers and layers of grim years, of decades that seemed even longer because of the tremendous amount that happened in them.

That was five years ago. In the meantime, Anastasia Maximova has completed her degree in Hispanic Language and Literature, worked as a tour guide, written her doctoral thesis on mechanisms for spreading subcultures, reached a highly respectable level in Catalan and translated many more stories by many more authors than those who appear in this anthology. She now works as a sworn legal translator.

My dilettante attitude restricts my knowledge of Russia, the U.S.S.R. and of Russian. Anastasia Maximova asked me to write this prologue despite my strange interactions with the embassy – that I will reveal shortly – and my ignorance of any of the issues and themes explored here. This prologue is mine but the choice of writers and stories was a joint affair. Some authors were left out of this first selection that we hope to publish in a sequel.

We have chosen writers who could bear witness to some of the events that have shaped the development of Russia and have reversed the conventional time sequence by starting with Ola Yevgueniyeva and ending with Jossef Bergchenko. The reader will find a Russia that is familiar, themes that speak to our most immediate present, experiences lived on the other side of Europe, far from here and yet right here. In the words of Anastasia Maximova, everything is translatable, "even language, even literature".

3.

My first contact with Russia was with the U.S.S.R. I now know that the U.S.S.R. wasn't Russia and that Russia wasn't the U.S.S.R.

At the time, however, there were things that belied such a perception. When I looked at a map, it seemed as if the red that marked the whole of that vast country, should spread everywhere and saturate, not only the republics, but also Comecon, and thus splash over into such remote spots as Cuba, Angola, the Yemen or Vietnam. Even its shape: Russia was like the main trunk that was extending its roots to the south and the whole of the world. Besides, there was the name, U.R.S.S. in Catalan, which out of sheer serendipity ended up resembling the name of the central country that dominated the rest.

We had a number of books at home on the Russian Revolution and Second World War. As well as a history of the post-war wars. All these books had excellent accompanying photos (an excellent range for a child living in Saidí almost thirty years ago). There was also *The Gulag Archipelago*, which easily balanced whatever was put on the other side of the scales.

Had I been a slightly more gullible child, I might have put a lot more things on the propaganda side. Readers may find this highly unlikely but, for a couple of years, from the age of nine to eleven, I had contact with the Russian Embassy in Madrid. Minimal contact; I sent letters and the embassy employees sent me books about the U.S.S.R. As I write this I think "how stupid could you have been", but the fact is I received booklets about the Soviet Union's scientific advances, aerospace power or wonderful health services. I say "booklets" because they were small format with equally small contents. The propaganda was so obvious that even I, a pre-adolescent, in Saidí, in 1982, could detect it. The Russian health services were magnificent, as was state education. Workers were awarded the status of heroes and the peoples of the U.S.S.R. co-existed in a folkloric harmony that prevented any kind of dissidence. Etcetera.

Nevertheless, I continued to be interested. I placed what films I received from the U.S.S.R. next to the film myths of the U.S.A. I remember buying a V.H.S. Russian version of "Treasure Island". It was a year after my exchanges with the embassy and coincided with the arrival in Saidí of a tramp who claimed to have visited Russia. He was no ordinary tramp. He was reasonably well dressed and accompanied by a dog, a wolfhound that obeyed instructions in three or four different languages. I hardly need to add how fascinating we found him and how sick he must have been of all those kids waiting to see the dog duck down and spring up at such strange words. Besides, he always had a tale to tell, about Poland, Czechoslovakia, and Russia . . . Had he really visited all those countries? I will never know, the tramp lived up to his name and disappeared.

Then I read what you would expect. Tolstoy, Chekhov, Pushkin . . . As the years passed, I added Platonov, Tsvetlaieva, Bunin and, above all, Bulgakov.

When I left Saidí, Russians, Lithuanians, Latvians, Poles, Romanians and Bulgarians started to arrive. Now Saidí is remote territory for me and gradually, as I have been writing all I have had to write, it has become a distant Russia, and now Saidí and I aren't what we used to be, Saidí is also slightly Russian.

4.

Mark Kharitonov, Boris Akunin, Vassili Ashionov, Vladimir Sorokin, Ludmila Ulitskaia and Mikhail Shishkin are some of the best known writers of contemporary literature today. The authors included in this anthology are part of one of the many underground currents in Russian fiction over the last hundred years. What remains of these writers? I don't know and would say that nobody knows, but I am certain that they have helped, in one way or another, to create this world that moves on from one set of writers to another and that they have left their trace. In the end, sooner or later, deep down or in the shallows all writers will go underground together with what they have written.

Ola Yevgueniyeva, Vera-Margarita Abanserev, Vitali Kroptkin,

Aleksandr Volkov and Jossef Bergchenko were unknown to me before Anastasia Maximova sent me their stories. I find they are a fiction about a fiction. Everything that happens in their stories in the end relates the story of a territory and a country that could be imaginary. Couldn't we, even in real life, come to believe that Russian history over the last century and a half was simply one huge fable? A country that is so vast its very existence seems a fabrication, epic events on an inconceivable scale, unleashing and suffering earthquakes that are felt the world over . . . And as if that fiction could only be understood in this way, these stories describe an arc of history that extends from that beginning of time that is the nineteenth century, to the era of low-cost flights. From the recreation of traditional fables to Russia's difficult relationship with the twentieth century. These stories speak of Russia from the inside, far from vogues that try to make places disappear into non-places or dissolve our subjectivities in societies in flux. They are physical, palpable stories, their characters don't suffer from existential anguish à la française, or servile irony, or that ubiquitous postmodernism that dissolves forms and identities . . . The stories we have chosen spring from a reality that has nothing in common with the distances imposed by metaliterature or any of the artefacts that have ruled the roost this side of the Wall, and throughout the last century. Plots and characters who interact and think, and real scenarios, as in stories by Maupassant, Chekhov or Salinger.

5.

In 1990, Viktor Erofeyev wrote that all the texts generated by the Soviet system, whether for or against, were behind the times and irrelevant, that Soviet literature had died a death, that it was almost buried, as would become evident over the next ten years to the year 2000, with the disappearance of the writer bureaucrats who had been supported by the

Party and the government. They may have their shaky moments that call for grandiloquent declarations to show they are even more dependent on what they are trying to distance themselves from, possibly quite blindly. Everything starts and finishes in the present, but there have always been writer bureaucrats and it is more than likely there will be for the next hundred years. Sometimes, the more bureaucratically servile they have been, the more revolutionary they have become, signing ever more radical articles and manifestos. As happens here and everywhere, I imagine revolutionary (sic), servile writer bureaucrats will be replaced by others that are equally servile, bureaucratic and revolutionary, philosophers without philosophy yet with eternal sinecures, and illustrious suicidal poets. In this respect, if we put this into proportion, Russia has been quite like other countries: these stories tend to level everyone down.

Similarly, we are alike when on the up and much that happens in these stories is interchangeable, the humanity of the characters, the scenarios and landscapes, and also the morality of the era in which they are located. Here and there, from one end of Europe to the other, countries under a dictator, nations and citizens under the boot of alien states, civil wars, communism and fascism, the exiled, the conformists and the adaptors . . . Stories are born, grow and transmute everywhere, simultaneously. But they don't die, that's why they travel from one town to another, from one country to another, even though, as in the case of the stories by Jossef Bergchenko or Aleksandr Volkov, they had been hidden so long we might have concluded they were lost for good.

Mikhail Bulgakov, to whose memory Anastasia Maximova and I would like to dedicate this book, said that manuscripts don't burn. I think that good books do burn, but like the burning bush, they never go out, and continue to warm and illuminate the here and now. Perhaps they spring from other times and distant countries, but they are heard by those who want to read them and if they have ears, they will listen.

As Anastasia Maximova says, everything is translatable, even language.

F. S. April 2009

OLA YEVGUENIYEVA

Ola Yevgueniyeva was born in Ossinovaia Rostcha in 1967. She studied law and worked as a lawyer for an important multinational company. She was awarded several grants and fellowships and after living in Sweden for two years was writer-in-residence at Boston University. She now works as a freelance journalist for a number of press agencies.

Her first book, White Nights, Grey Days, earned her a reputation as one of the most representative voices of her generation and some critics were of the view that the book initiated the new St Petersburg short story. The four stories selected are from The Nevski Prospect Might Not Be Long Enough, a collection of stories of affairs of the heart and everyday amorous triangles, drenched in the urban reality that surrounds them. The longings of the characters take the reader into a Russia that manages to be at once contemporary and timeless. Her novel, and most recent book, as this anthology is being published, The Flight of Free Men, has revived the polemic about the mechanics of corruption that allowed Communist Party leaders to prosper unexpectedly through their manipulation of the contacts and structures of the old regime and the opportunities new times have provided. Ola Yevgueniyeva is currently working on a series of articles on the world of work in Russia that are appearing in publications in the United States.

LOW-COST LIFE, LOW-COST LOVE

A customer is bawling at me but I smile back as if he'd said you're lovely. I'm Raïssa and work as an air hostess, though I don't fly now, I'm ground staff.

The customer is still shouting. According to Jelena, my friend behind the counter, there are two kinds of customer: those who shout and those who say nothing.

It's also true, as she quite rightly said, that there are winners and losers. If there are people who stuff their lunches and others who peck like birds, she says there are two kinds of people, those who'd eat the world and those who'd throw it on the rubbish tip, even if it was against the rules. In a word, whenever there is any doubt, the two extremes, never a shade of grey. You know, the coffee can be sweet or not so sweet, with a spot of sugar or really bitter, but it will always be excellent or like tar. If there's a problem with a customer, she'll wink at me and mutter he's a pain, or if a smart, handsome young man walks by, he's a darling.

It is a long time since this customer was a handsome lad and he's still bawling at me. Hey, you know, now we've gone off the boil, guys are pains or darlings, and we don't have time for much else. If there's a hitch at the airport, she grouses and grumbles and then, as gutsy as could be, pounds her hips or pounds the table and says: "There are two kinds of planes. Ours and the rest."

She also says there are two kinds of airport, ours and the European sort. When computers crash, there are German and Russian systems, and depending which, either they sort it straight away or you can start doing it manually . . .

The customer goes. Jelena gives his back the finger and I follow suit. Jelena . . . We've been working together for three years. She came from the airport in Minsk, she always says that when she came to St Petersburg she said there were airports and "airports". Before Minsk she'd worked at the one in Vitebsk. There are airports, terrible airports and aerodromes for biplanes that spread pesticides, where Tupolevs still land.

On this basis, her philosophy of life is as clear as water, white or black, good or bad, Moscow or St Petersburg. Europe or Russia, expensive or cheap, rich or poor . . .

There used to be the three of us, Jelena, Gala and me. The three of us behind the counter, but they made Gala a flight hostess after six months and we continued as ground staff. Yes, you've guessed, there are two kinds of hostesses, according to Jelena, those who fly and those who are grounded and aren't even halfway to being air hostesses.

We now work on the ground for low-cost companies. For the last three years we've been arguing over the weight of suitcases, checking wrong tickets and dealing with ladies who are sick after gorging in St Petersburg and have to change their flights. Our check-in counters don't have sweets or pens with the company crest ("I swear there are two kinds of company!") but we have plenty in a little box that a flight attendant working for Lufthansa gave us. In that sense, says Jelena, they *are* all the same, all flight attendants are gay.

Jelena gives me a look. Toilet. Gives me another look. It means she needs to go to the toilet even though there's a very long queue. As soon as she comes out from behind the counter, everybody will start to say where's she off to, we're in a hurry and the planes won't wait etc.

"I can't wait."

I flex all the muscles in my face and neck and put on my broadest smile and act like the nicest person in the world in order to defuse all the complaints, but even so, some people shout. Those who shout and those who don't, as usual.

A passenger demands a seat in the tail. Those seats are the safest, apparently, he read it in some study or other. Fine, in the tail, next to the toilet. He must repeat the same story whenever he's being checked in and rate the hostesses according to the answers he gets. How boring.

Before I've given her a second thought, I see her rushing back as if she were in the Olympics. We're banned from running in the airport so nobody gets nervous, or thinks there's been a breakdown or that that hostess is running from a plane with a serious problem or worse. She sits down and the queue starts to shorten again. They'll all be gone within the hour. And we'll stretch out, making sure no-one notices, and catch up on our sleep.

Ours is a small counter between S.A.S. and other low-cost companies. The other side of S.A.S., it's the upper class, Lufthansa, K.L.M. and all the others that supply their hostesses proper uniforms and not these polyester sack-cloths that fray everywhere. Jelena and I sometimes fantasise about marrying those smart guys on their way to the British Airways lounge, who must be engineers contracted by an oil firm or experts in natural gas, with a house in London, one here in St Petersburg and a beautiful residence in Kola, in the oilfields, so cool, and us inside those big huts that look nothing special from the outside and that inside are palaces with saunas, jacuzzi and all kinds of things . . . And then the old cow who misread her ticket knocks on the counter and brings us back to our low-cost lives.

We knock off at two and the next shift starts. The idiots always complain we've put the chairs too high, or that there are too many forms to fill, or about some label that has been mislaid that they have to waste time finding, but we laugh once we've pressed the lever that goes *pafffff* and leaves the seat as high as it can go, and mix up the forms . . . Anything for a laugh.

Two o'clock! Two o'clock! Ding-dong, rings the clock, imitating a church bell!

Jelena won't be coming home with me today, she's staying overnight at a girlfriend's because we have a guest at our place. My guest. I've not mentioned that we live together. On the first nights one of us has a guy to sleep over, the other doesn't show. Besides, she's in no mood for jokes, as she's still not got over her last break-up.

"Did I say how fucking envious I am?"

"After number fourteen?" I laugh.

"And did I ask you to make sure he doesn't leave his hair in the basin or the shower?"

"My last guy was the hairy one."

"Ah, so he was," she laughs, trying to provoke me.

The way to get over our hang-ups – the one I'm now trying out – is to make them more visible.

Her family lives south of Minsk. In fact, she sees more of mine than hers. Her mother – the long-suffering, eternal divorcée with a chip on her shoulder – says we should get married, that it's not frowned on anymore, and that the two of us could do well out of it. The last time she said that to us, Jelena replied she'd been single for longer than she'd been married, that she'd think about it, that some like men and others like women . . . Her mother almost choked when she heard that.

Now Jelena is stressed. When I came back from changing she stared at me and scratched her nose hard. When she does that, it means she is stressed out. I felt the same when she was with Max. I imagine it's quite

normal, a friend of ours who is a psychologist told us we needed secur-
ity, and that by living together we had created a form of dependency
bonding. Dependency bonding, you buy this and I'll buy that, you
get dinner ready today and I'll do it tomorrow . . . make yourself scarce
when my new boyfriend comes because I'll do the same for you . . .
That must be it, bonding and all that jazz from when the bottle of
vodka shaped liked a sofa went to our heads . . . Bonding, the three of
us singing on our balcony, most likely.

In fact, we've often said that the best for both of us would be to find
a boyfriend now, at a party, or a work meeting, and then lead our lives
along parallel lines, but we both know this isn't possible. She waves
goodbye from the other bus stop, some people catch taxis, others, like
us, catch buses, our pay doesn't stretch any further. One day Jelena
stuck her face up against the window, clearly watering at the mouth, as
some United Airlines hostesses climbed into the limo van that was
their taxi, with a step that came down automatically. We had a girlfriend who one day, when a huge Lexus drove past that forced all us
pedestrians to step back, said we should be proud as she was that as
a country we had such wealthy compatriots, because it meant the
country was moving forward.

I ask you! I have a date at five in Tara Brooch and it's not the café
where I was hoping to have what might be a vital date. That is, the one
Niko thinks will give him the right to have supper and to eat me whole.
It all depends, as Jelena says, on the extras, because everything in life
is low-cost, at least for us, in St Petersburg, and life starts to get better
on the basis of extras, as we can't lead our lives in first class. When she
starts to say that outside St Petersburg and Moscow life isn't even low-
cost, she means she is really depressed and mentally back in Vitebsk!

But what can I do, she's just like that! I'm not depressed, though I
would have preferred to go to the Moscow Hotel – I love hotel bars, and

Tara Brooch hardly rates, but that's what there is. I'd have preferred it if Stepan had hung on longer. He went to Milan, and in Milan the Italian girls will be all over him. Stepan must have taken Milan by storm . . . but I still love him a bit, and if I'd not known he was sleeping with them, perhaps every other weekend, or once a month, or every two months, whenever . . . I'd have acted as if it was business as usual . . . But he upped and left. To Milan, and compared to all this and these uniforms that fluff up and itch . . . Jelena and I looked at the shops in Milan on the Internet and imagined we were the customers there . . . Bah, it's better not to . . . From silks and leathers to this bus's wooden seats . . . Stepan . . .

The truth is it's not this bus's wooden seats that rile me, what really makes me furious – rather than upsetting me – is recalling that Niko also wants a low-cost relationship, something that doesn't commit him here while he's working out how to get that job in Finland he's always talking about and only knows about through his cousin. If he says yet again how Finland sounds like a dream world I will get up and go. I still hardly know him. He doesn't work in the airport anymore, he's in a bank, but earning less money, a good move, that! Sure, I can see that signalling to aeroplanes isn't much fun, that going out on the landing strip in winter, with all the fumes from the planes and everything else . . . At least he's in the warm in the bank, but for less money and now he's taking me to Tara Brooch . . . He must think I'm an idiot and that the road to my bed starts in Finland, that I'll be dying to join him because you can bet we'll both end up working in an office for Nokia. Pull the other one!

Jelena sends me a text. She found a dress that was really reduced and has bought me a present. And whether it's still Tara Brooch, and if he then takes me to the Umbrov, I should say I've got a headache. "If Umbrov headache. Dirty. Finland not worth it. Haha." "If Umbrov nasty tomorrow, breakfast together?" and I get a laconic "O.K." for an answer and she rings off.

I'd like it to turn out fine. I know it's more likely to fail because poor Niko hasn't much to offer and I've not much to offer in return. Then I think . . . On the one hand, the world around me has nothing better to give me. Neither my world nor his has much to offer and we try to grab what we can. On the other hand, Niko might have the spark that makes life a little bit more liveable, at least open a window in an attic near the clouds . . . I'm blathering like a fool, but I like to allow myself the luxury of blathering like a fool. Or is that banned from our low-cost lives?

Our *whole* world is totally low-cost. My mother sometimes says, when I'm complaining, that this is our fate, whoever's in power, predictable as the needle of a compass, even though you turn it round, the needle keeps pointing you in the same direction because as things stand you've not got the magnet that can drive it crazy, that could put your life in your hands, or at your feet, better still. On my way to Tara Brooch, at a traffic light, the bus hits the usual pothole. All the drivers do, the one who is going to Burg-Burg as well, you feel the bus juddering and it hits the bottom of your spine and shakes every vertebra up to your neck.

I can see him in the entrance to Tara Brooch. He's no great shakes, but then I look at myself and know I'm no great shakes either, a low-cost groundhostess. What more can I expect? The bus stop is past the corner of the street, he hasn't seen me yet, I could decide not to get off, the foliage of the plants in the pots by the entrance provide camouflage, I could turn tail, say they changed my shift, make some excuse to call the whole thing off. He goes to a local barber and the clothes he is wearing are hardly right for a first date . . . I have at least changed. I've been carrying my bag around carefully all day, making sure not to crease what is my second best set of clothes, though not my best. When I went out with Stepan, I wore two garments Saskia let me have and nothing could seem too good, but with Niko, it was as if I'd anticipated everything on the cards and had dressed accordingly.

Better turn tail, though I'm spoiling nothing if I have a try. He may be a good sort, better than he looks. I mean, as if anyone has ever asked my opinion about how to dress. Nobody apart from Jelena ever has.

And if he starts on about Finland . . . I expect Helsinki airport is better than ours here.

I look at myself in the shop window. I should have asked Saskia to lend me something.

THE RUSSIAN DOLLS' HOUSE

In 1957, the census official asked the old man:

"Where were you born, Ivan Ivanovitch?"

And he replied:

"In St Petersburg, sir."

"Where did you grow up, Ivan Ivanovitch?" the official then asked.

"In Petrograd, sir."

The official continued with his questionnaire:

"And where do you live now?"

"In Leningrad, sir."

The census official asked him one last question:

"And where would you like to live, Ivan Ivanovitch?"

And Ivan Ivanovitch bowed his head:

"In the St Petersburg my mother told me about, sir, if that's possible."

PIOTR JOSEF OHRENMANN

Diary of an Estonian Bewildered by the World and Mankind

She phoned me the previous night. Ever since we met I've known the phone may ring at any time of the day or night.

"Juri, Juri, I must talk to you."

"Maia, it's . . ."

"Juri, I must talk to you, we must talk . . ."

"For heaven's sake, I won't ask you if you know what time it is because I know you do, Maia," I replied, coming round as my alarm

35

clock hit the ground, its back came off and the batteries rolled under my bed.

"Come on, Juri, you're not doing anything vital and you're not with anyone, or you wouldn't have your phone switched on. Tell them at work that they needed you at home, and I'll tell Father."

"Maia, I'm asleep . . ."

"Come on, Juri, we can have a coffee at eleven, go for a walk and then have lunch together, go on, say yes, Juri, I'll tell Father to let work know, come on, Juri, I'm depending on you, you know?"

She always persuades me in a flash. We've known each other for fifteen years, since we were eighteen, fifteen years ago I was the most ridiculously in love youth ever encountered and couldn't say no to her. She is the prettiest woman in the whole of St Petersburg, with a doll's face that makes you perform like a puppet.

And, obviously, the puppet rang work to say he couldn't go in that morning, and walked along Nevski Prospect as far as the Neva, then four more streets to her house.

The house where she still lives is on Vassilevski Island, near the palace. And she lives there, just like her house, as if the years go by and make them more attractive, as if time passes and doesn't spoil her face or its façade, but lends them a gentler, more pleasant veneer. The steps to the house lead down to the road in an elegant, leisurely, arresting style, as if they were really a red carpet. Whenever I went, I wondered how that stairway could possibly have survived all those revolutions and wars, occupations and bombs. It looked as if it had been preserved in a bell jar. The first time she invited me I went up and down the steps seven or eight times until I heard the butler cough. As for the house, you'd soon get lost inside, the entrance, the reception area, then the white gilded doors to a lobby with two marble staircases to the anteroom on the first floor. My God, you feel as if you're in a museum purpose built to display the family's good taste: nothing jars and it lacks nothing in terms of paintings, fireplaces and statues. Maia was expecting me and had coffee served in the conservatory. Oh, and there are women who spend a fortune on the most expensive clothes and women – Maia being one of them – who will never be as elegant as when she walks downstairs in her negligée and towel. The St Petersburg aristocracy, 100 per cent pure-bred over heaven knows how many generations that have survived the Tsars, the Communists and the mafias. Like the house: business as usual.

When I saw her rushing ahead of the servant to open the door, I began to think it must be something urgent.

"Hey, Maia, how do you know I sometimes disconnect?" I asked her.

"Don't ask me and I won't tell you any lies."

"Come on, Maia, tell me! How do you know when I disconnect?" You always have to persist with Maia.

"When you were with Irina, it was always engaged, you couldn't have been on the phone so long."

"So how do you know how long I'm on the phone to Irina for? Did you bug my phone? Is that how you spend your time, my love?"

"I just did my sums, I know what you earn and what calls cost, that's easy enough, isn't it?"

"Alright, touché, but don't play policeman with me, and tell me what's the matter now. Did you tell your father to ring Fetissov?"

Fetissov is my boss, and is under orders from her father. Whenever his daughter wants to see me they have to ring him to say I need the day off. Fetissov hates me, but I find him amusing, he reacts like those dogs that bark from the other side of the gate and hurl themselves at the fence when you just laugh to annoy them. Her father found me that job. In fact, she did. It's an import–export company that controls part of the port and the airport.

We've known each other for fifteen years, from the day when I pretended she'd knocked me over driving her car. I pretended to fall off my bicycle and lose consciousness. I revealed all a month later and she bawled at me, "You're crazy, you're crazy!" and swore she would change university and go abroad to study. "You're crazy! You're crazy!" But she didn't, nor did she tell anyone it had all been a ploy to catch her. From that point on, we've been the closest of close, I've always been in love with her and she'd say I was her best friend. A thousand-ton lorry crushed my heart whenever she said that.

"Yes, I've told him, don't go on so." She got up for a moment, sat down again, her legs under her. "Juri, I have something I must tell you. Juri, this time I do really think I'm going to get married. This time it's for real."

"For real? To that butcher?" I asked, imitating the tone of voice she uses when she is lecturing me or relating something important.

"Yes, to that butcher, if you must keep calling him that. I'd like to remind you that he is the owner of the second biggest meat company in the country."

"Do you want me to act as best man or chaplain?" I'd gone too far, that was clear.

"Don't be sarcastic, that's the last thing I need, my love, let's drink our coffee, then go for lunch at our place."

"Hey, not so fast, dear."

"Alright, let's begin again. I think I am going to get married. I'm not absolutely sure, but I think that marrying Alexei isn't exactly the end of the world. It might even be amusing and good for me. After all, I can always have a lover, like Mother, like Grandmother, like Great-Grandmother. And he will have his too, and won't bother me, Mother says the headache excuse still works really well," she laughed, and I wasn't exactly amused, but she was laughing, I imagine, to make the situation seem more tolerable. "She says it's easier if you each do it with your lover than have to create close bonds and all that . . ."

"And I imagine that as we're being so frank about everything I can ask whether I can be your lover?"

"Aren't you already?" she smiled. There's not another smile like hers in the whole world. It must come from the fact that the ladies of St Petersburg have been polishing their smiles ever since the French taught them how.

"Yes, but I mean in a stable way, you know. We'll see each other every day and eat out and Alexei can pay, and I'll be chauffeur."

"Mmm . . . that's a possibility," she laughed again. "My mother had a liaison with our teacher. Now, I don't see you acting as the teacher of my sons and daughters, particularly my daughters. I'd be so afraid . . . On the other hand, maybe Alexei has dealings with the mafia, and you ought to be afraid . . ."

We had endured several long periods of separation as a result of more or less longstanding commitments. She knew better than I did that it wasn't at all likely it could ever have worked for us; my realism was less cheerful, and more resigned. At the very least, her father would have disinherited her. And as I didn't have any way to earn a living for the moment we simply kept playing along. Obviously neither of us was getting any younger. Local suitors were marrying off, and from what she told me about what her father was saying, decisions couldn't be delayed much longer. In the meantime we had enjoyed all the wild adventures her parents turned a blind eye to, knowing full well they would do whatever they wanted with her. We had driven as far as Paris in her mother's car and holidayed there for two weeks; they knew I had a key to their little girl's studio apartment, on the other side of the Neva, they even knew we had planned to go to New York, and heaven knows where else. And the truth is I would have done whatever she decided, but I knew she didn't belong to my world, she doesn't, she can only act the part, adopt a disguise; she belongs to that place where things cannot change. St Petersburg is still called St Petersburg, and the inertia in these families' behaviour is stronger than any force levered by any political change that tries to subvert them, as if the refined way to hold the handle of a cup of coffee was more powerful than any political situation or historical upheaval.

The maid wasn't there, so I stood up and kissed her.

"You know, perhaps I'll go to bed with him in advance so it's not such a big shock for you. I should really give you a little shock because it's what you deserve for treating me so badly." And she smiled again.

Oh, the refinement of the St Petersburg upper classes. You will never drink such excellent coffee again. As soon as she looked at me over the cup and opened her eyes, I realised it was for real this time. She must have planned all this, planned this down to that night-time call, even her eyes peering above the cup of coffee, porcelain behind porcelain, all pre-planned, so I couldn't hurt her, so-I-couldn't-hurt-her, though a twelve-axle lorry was squashing my heart.

I imagine – we both imagined far too much – that I saw it was inevitable. We had both had a lot of short-lived relationships set up to stoke jealousy, or when she went abroad, to London . . . She went off for a whole year to see whether we would forget one another, and though we are still lamenting that decision, love welded us together from afar, it was as if a towrope that left the golf courses in St Petersburg and Finland, crossed the Baltic, turned across Kattegat and Skagerrak, passed over the North Sea, entered the Thames estuary till it reached her flat in the centre. In her letters, she called it the umbilical cord. Well, you know, this umbilical cord started to grow from the day I pretended she had knocked me off my bicycle, and had never slackened once.

Maia stood up and removed the towel that was wrapped around her hair, her sopping white dressing gown and towel, my turbaned princess. She gathered her hair up and looked at me. She gave me her hand and told me to follow her. I had been inside her house several times. They invited me to supper after the collision. They weren't used to sharing their table and conversing with someone who didn't belong to their social class and the whole dinner was perfectly polite and cold. After dinner we transferred to the library, the first private library I had ever seen. In the centre was a globe of the world as tall as I was and above that a grandiose chandelier, and the whole house had been fashioned in a similar style. Marble stairs and fine woods, and all that furniture seemed to crystallise the good habits of St Petersburg from the day it was founded. To walk through that house was to take a walk through the history of Russia: furniture from every era and portraits and paintings in highly ornate frames, their titles on gilded plaques.

At the time Maia's father was the head of a company that exported raw materials and imported manufactured goods, one of the most lucrative and least regulated businesses I had ever seen. I saw it close-up because I worked there. He had been a leading member of the Party in St Petersburg, a man with lots of links and contacts in Moscow and with the Party committees that controlled the port and the airport. The thousands of tons processed in the '70s and '80s turned into thousands of millions of dollars in the '90s and he was always in the right place at the right time.

I had lost count, and so had Maia, of the huge number of director-ships and vice-chairmanships that he held and the number of boards he belonged to or chaired. He even had a team of accountants to check on his accountants, Maia would laugh, and often tell me, in high-risk reve-lations, about the changes being introduced, the proceeds from which her father always managed in a way that benefited the companies and his own family. "If he could survive the Party, surviving capitalism will be child's play for him, that's what he always says," she would reply when I noted activity that looked as if it might undermine everything and asked, "What will your father do now?"

"Keep cool and calm and win out, as ever," she would answer.

Her mother married him when the two families that controlled the Party in St Petersburg decided there wasn't room for anyone else and that it was better to reach an accord so no outsider could poke his nose in. Moscow gave the green light, and lo and behold, the gorgeous Maia married Nikita and from then on they were known as the Tsar and Tsarina of St Petersburg. Everybody knew about the problems between her mother and father, including her younger sister and her, but it was very strange, because nobody who had climbed that wonderful staircase, that staircase that had never been affected by fires or bombing raids or rebellions, that staircase that took you to the entrance, to reception and to the bottom of the inside staircase, nobody would have thought anything could challenge the order that reigned there so unperturbed, ancient luxury, as ancient and soothing as the soft, gentle sound of the footsteps on the carpet adorning the stairway.

The top. The top was forbidden territory. I had never climbed that high. Her mother would say that lovers should never come as far as the bedrooms. The family bedrooms.

Her mother: Madame Maia was a unique, inimitable lady, way beyond whatever she reproduced. The women of the household had given their daughters all they needed to maintain their status, ineffable beauty and foxy cunning guided by the selfish gene, which certainly does exist; the women belonging to that family surely possessed the proof that some scientists are searching for: here genetics perpetuates all. In the portrait in the lobby you cross to go upstairs you find evidence on a black background. No Lempicka imitations here, simply genuine St Petersburg 1960s rococo. A woman who can have her portrait painted against a dark background next to a blossoming almond tree will always have my respect and we should pay homage to her. Maia's face has emerged from the same mould as her mother's. Men have killed each other fighting over these faces on the street corners of St Petersburg, Verona, Troy, everywhere since the world has existed. When you look into those eyes, you feel the spears that pierced the hearts of rejected suitors.

At the top. The curtains are French and the furniture, collectors' items. That is where you find her parents' bedroom, the guest bedrooms, the biggest bathrooms you have ever seen, from the time when her father purchased the house next door and refurbished it as an annexe. She walked in front barefoot over the carpets. There are women who are more elegant in a bathrobe than others who parade their haute couture. Breeding will out, I suppose.

"Come on," she said, "in here."

We entered a bedchamber. A huge bed and ottoman in one corner. The curtains gleamed like silk in the light from the huge picture windows. Books and paintings on the walls, and a bureau littered with a mass of antique black and white photos.

"Stretch out here while I put something on," and she left me stretched out on the ottoman. She took my shoes off and put some vespers on the record player. Never C.D.s, she liked the background buzz, like the little noises you hear at a concert.

It was her mother's private bedroom. Nobody else could cross that threshold, but she was away for the day. She had thought it all through, even the surprise effect, and all I could do was watch everything unfold, quite unable to do anything to change what was about to happen. The room had everything a woman could want, from perfumes to a pair of amazing mirrors. Oh, those mirrors! When she came back, in an

43

unbelted, cream-coloured dress, its neckline embroidered with flowers, she sat next to me on the ottoman.

"Of course," she said, "you have *never* been right to the top. If my mother discovered you had been here with me, she would kill you. You, not me, right, because I am the apple of her eye. Look at these paintings."

The walls were hung with portraits of women from different periods, by different painters, in changing styles and poses, although you could detect a family air, a gesture, the same feline look, a naïveté at once contrived and persuasive, the same dazzlingly white delicate skin and rosy cheeks. There you are, I thought, the distillation of the lineage you love, now you see how these women act. There were two on the other wall, two women who looked as if they wanted to shake hands.

"No, don't look at them, they are two ugly aunts, and more than a hundred and fifty years old. Look at the one over here. My great-great-grandmother married an industrialist who traded with Swedes and Poles. Coal and iron ore, once he had seen how the returns on wood weren't as high as he wanted, if he had to deal in iron ore, then so be it. My great-great-grandmother had eight daughters and three sons. Look at that," she said, pointing to a photograph above the bureau, "they all look quite different. My great-great-grandfather and his sons and daughters were as alike as chalk and cheese. My mother pointed that out to me about a year ago."

She took a breath and then resumed.

"The next one is my great-grandmother, they used to call her Catherine the Great, because she was always giving orders. Married to the count, you know which. One of the wealthiest men in the whole of Russia. They said she had more furs in her house than in the whole of Siberia. Her trysts with her captain were sung about throughout St Petersburg. Mother still has copies of some of the verses. It is well known she gave the orders, but never said anything, nobody ever knew what she was thinking. Oh, my dear, I don't know anything about that, ask the count, he is the one who does . . ." Maia got up to point out the portrait of the count, a surly-looking fellow, a forebear to Fetissov, perhaps. "He didn't marry until he was thirty-five, and when everybody thought he would be a lifelong bachelor, he goes and lands the best catch in the whole of St Petersburg, Catherine the Great." Maia was gesticulating wildly and seemed to be so happy to be able to tell me all these stories in her mother's private bedchamber. She'd get up from the ottoman and come back, dancing as she walked. Too happy; luckily I knew her and could imagine what was coming.

"My grandmother Sophia, look at her, a mere child."

In effect, a lovely child, a perfect portrait of Maia painted sixty years before Maia was born, an extremely refined, strong face, as if all the other portraits had shed their blemishes and established a canon that couldn't be broken, mother and granddaughter, faithful reproductions of the model, same eyes, hair and look. I knew her grandmother's story as well as I knew her mother's, as she had recounted both to me. She married one of the officers who settled in St Petersburg after the revolution.

"She is the key factor in our family, everything was going to rack and ruin and she managed to save it," she said, her back to me, leaning on the bureau, "the house, the papers that enabled my father to reclaim land and other property and, above all, a stability for our family that means we don't have to worry about a thing. Of course, she opened her legs to any man who could give her something, and finally married my mother to my father . . . Grandmother . . ."

But it was too late. She talked and talked and didn't turn round. With her back to me, quiet, all her previous cheerfulness had vanished. She was crying, and when she cried, she didn't want anyone to see her.

I know she had cried a lot before she rang me and had hoped she wouldn't on the day she told me she was marrying Alexei, but she did what all those ladies must have done before her, those dolls who declared they bore the breath that carries from mother to daughter and keeps the house safe against whatever wind is blowing. A fresh, invigorated breath like the one I still find today when I kiss my beloved Maia.

"Maia, I love you," I said.

"And I love you too, and will always, but you must go now, Mother could be back any minute. I will ring you. I promise not to reproach you anymore if I find the phone is disconnected."

That was all ten years ago. I try not to disconnect my phone and she now rings me frequently and waits for me in her study on the other side of the Neva.

There is a new picture on the staircase in her house. She is standing in the middle of a park with a lot of people in the background behind her. In the distance, level with her heart, a cyclist is about to crash to the ground.

LIFE IN MINIATURE ON THE M-18

Aleksandr runs through the scrub, as he does every day. The school bus isn't in sight yet and will be here in a couple of minutes. He lifts up a stone slab and carefully unravels plastic bags that are wrapped round a pair of shoes. He rubs them with a cloth from yet another bag and then hides the boots he's been wearing up until then and he will wear to retrace his steps home in the afternoon.

As soon as he has tied his laces – perfect, matching, exemplary bows – he walks to the crossroads taking care not to dirty them. Standing on that stone he had dragged to the side of the road, he looks a picture, not a spot of mud, no dry earth, not a speck of dust, beautifully ironed, and gleaming parting and shoes. Even though it rained yesterday, bag in hand, he looks like a statue on his pedestal.

The school bus stops. Aleksandr gets in, greets Mrs Gromoshka and sits in seat eighteen, next to the aisle, right behind her and across from number fifteen, where *she* sits. Where she will sit. It's two stops before she gets on. His day begins when the doors open and she climbs in.

Will she laugh again today too when she sees him? Will she have plaits? And wear a hairpin? Or a ponytail? And that headscarf he likes when she wears it round her neck . . . He has occasionally spoken to her, but so far has always got it wrong. He spoke to her one day when Putin appeared on the telly practising judo in combat with another judoka who was continually hitting the ground. He asked her whether she had seen the president, but she replied that her father didn't like Putin, and he quickly removed his name from the list for the training sessions to try for a belt the colour of which he has now completely forgotten. This made her even more fascinating: her father didn't like Putin and she dared tell the other kids.

However, for the first time in the two years that they have been doing that journey together to school, she isn't there. She's not standing at the end of the path that runs down from her house, and the bus stops and waits for five seconds with the doors shut, then drives off relentlessly and his world collapses. His heart clatters more than the bus windows, or the Russian pennants flapping against the driver's side.

Mrs Gromoshka also clatters and shakes as the bus bumps and jolts along. The boy sitting in the seat in front is eternally punished. He too makes a din and Mrs Gromoshka has assigned him this place until he goes to university. There are two boys who are discussing their history lesson holding their text books, the usual that happens on a bus, but the rest is simply St Petersburg in the distance, passing cars, the remains of the snow that the rain that has restarted hasn't yet turned to slush, and this dark grey sky that enters his heart and sends him into a spin.

What if she's ill? Flu? Tonsillitis? A week not seeing her will seem like forever. What if she has changed school? A lot of kids have recently. Could he ask to change school? His parents had already had to struggle to send him to this one rather than the "reformatory" next to the factory. His father tells his mother not to call the school that, though he reckons that "'reformatory' lets that dreadful place off lightly". How many questions could race through his brain in a second? She had been there before, a minute ago when all he could think about was his shoes and everything he was dragging behind him. All this time he had been thinking how he had been trailing in his wake an invisible burden of projects that committed him to her and the world. He had been making plans. He had been studying hard and been included in the photo of the best pupils at the Patriarchs' School, was one of the most visible during the school festival, and had thought of bringing the press cuttings of his grandfather who had been a Labour Hero; he had joined the water-polo squad because she is in the swimming team. After walking more than a kilometre along a muddy path, he jumped on the bus pretending his parents had driven him to the crossroads, all just so she wouldn't give him that look she gave him the day a car splattered him.

However, at the next stop, the miracle happened just as he had thought all was lost: she climbs into the bus. Mrs Gromoshka asks where she's off to, soaked like that, how come she is so late, while the kid who is always naughty tries to lean his elbow on the back of his seat so it hits her when she walks past. She says they overslept and luckily her father had been able to run fast enough to catch the bus before it entered the M-18 to St Petersburg. Aleksandr imagines her father, and how they must have rushed hell for leather to catch the bus, her mother making her sandwich in a desperate hurry, the snatched kisses . . .

Nadia walks down the aisle and sits in her usual seat and the sun shines for him, and not just for a moment, and lights up everything, the road and St Petersburg, the snow and the puddles, the mud and the cement on the dirty grey buildings, when she asks him – yes, him! – if he has a handkerchief and she smiles and says she is very sorry he has to see her like that in those wet clothes and dirty shoes.

THE FORFEIT

"A castle, a prancing, whinnying horse, a bishop, and the queen and king, and the same on the other wing, bishop, horse and castle. In front, a row of pawns. Confronting them, on the other side of the board, the black pieces in the same formation. Look, the powerful are in the middle, protected by the cleverer, more scheming pieces, those that move diagonally and cut into your flank like a dagger when you're least expecting them, do you see? In a sword-like movement, an elegant thrust, sharp as the hats they wear, that are called mitres. The horses move like animals, two steps forward and one to the side, as if trotting sideways, they are animals, and don't think, and that's why they are so awkward. In contrast, the castles are buildings constructed by highly intelligent men, architects, and do you see how their vertical sides would collapse if they weren't built properly, their straight, perpendicular towers blocking streets and crushing buildings. Look how we set one in each corner and how the whole terrain, the whole battlefield, is a perfect square, and men, if they are going to move, need to mark out the territory and create their own routes, as in the streets of a city."

She listens in rapt attention. She doesn't know how or why she has ended up sitting on the other side of his table. She went for a stroll and after walking in the park for a while she sat down at the chess-player's table. The man asked her if she knew how to play, and she said they had taught them a little at school.

"We must open up the front line, the pieces behind don't want to remain behind that wall, they are pushing and shoving. Walls always have to be knocked down, everyone wants to expand, it is as if each of the two sides wants to conquer the whole earth and sea, it's like the world, do you see the parallel lines and the meridians? This board is the whole world, we men map out the earth so we know where we are, know what land we still have to conquer, do you see? When men are locked in at close quarters, they argue all the time. Here they are black and white, but colour is unimportant, the greatest differences are the ones you don't see."

He takes a breath and moves one of his pieces. She continues to listen.

"Now you are witnessing one of the most important moments. As soon as the line is broken, there is no stopping, the second the first piece is moved, there is no going backwards. Once the line is broken, it has to be broken completely, and the game and the battle only end when one of the sides can kill the other's king. Do you see? There is no such thing as a draw: stalemate is only a subterfuge to regroup forces and start all over again, a truce that ends when they start off again. We set out the pieces, as if the army had recovered its lines and was ready to join battle again. The pieces are a real joy to see when they are lined up, a real joy. What lies in between, is the space occupied by men, look, they're in dispute again, the only way to ensure there is an infinite stalemate is for the pawns not to break their lines, for the horses not to jump out and provoke the others, but by now you must have learned that perpetual peace is a silly notion, the desire always remains to possess territory and get rid of the foe. And the only way to do that and be able to move untrammelled is to kill, kill them all, if you can conquer them and only kill the king, fine; but, obviously . . . sometimes a massacre is the only way. Don't be scared, don't look at me like that, it is only a game."

The girl looks at him, for days she's been watching him and the chessboard set out on one of the tables, and today, after walking in the park as on so many afternoons, she has finally dared approach him. He likes playing, but is always by himself and seems a strange character. The other players are afraid of him, and although it's only a game, he takes lots of risks, and would rather lose than accept a stalemate. Rumour has it that he was an international grandmaster, that he competed abroad. But obviously, nobody knows for certain and nobody dares ask. The girl looks at him, but she's not afraid like the other players in the park, who don't know why they fear him, even though sometimes he does lose, not very often and because he takes too many risks. Maybe it is the cruel, heartless way he sacrifices his pieces, that are only pieces after all, or maybe it is his solitary state that puts people off.

"There are lots of ways you can play," he continues, "you can play by waiting for your opponent to make mistakes, some people only defend and others only attack, some are always afraid and others are never afraid, but nobody ever wants to lose their king, do you see the king there?" he asks, pointing at the piece and rolling it along with his fingertips. "It is at once the most valuable and the weakest piece, the king rises above the rest so they can all see who he is, but he needs everyone else's support if he doesn't want to fall, do you see, the other pieces are like bulwarks that must keep him standing, look, even the queen, who is tall as he is, may be sacrificed at any moment to save him. They are cowardly kings, who hide behind a line of pawns or exhaust their cavalry by making them rush up and down to upset the enemy's game. Yes, no need to look at me like that: the enemy is always the enemy. Do you see, the king can always go where he wants because he is the one who gives the orders, but he can only move one square because he is burdened down by his clothes and jewels, because he needs his retinue if he is going to move. Doesn't it strike you as strange that the queen can go everywhere and please herself and the king can only shuffle one step at a time?" The girl glances around, the other players also look at them, look at them as if afraid something might happen. "They think it's only a game, but it isn't, do you see the way the infantry is falling? Do you see how the horses are panting? They are exhausted, cornered, or perhaps the soldiers won't let them run away and they have been trapped in a blind alley, you can see how enclosed the terrain is, if it weren't, they'd all run away and hide in some other corner of the world. But, do you see? Do you see how they are filling the streets with rubbish from the castle turrets, and do you see how the castles collapse when they blow up their walls? The bishops are really agitated, and if the battle continues nothing will remain at the end, the desire to kill one's foe is so strong that those who succeed in crossing enemy terrain, who nothing can stop from humiliating the enemy, *are* promoted, and do you know what this promotion is about? Well, it is about being stronger and able to kill more ruthlessly, as simple as that. Look, do you see those grandads playing on that table? Do you see them? Do you see how they keep the other person's pieces behind theirs, as if they were prisoners? But this is only a game, don't think it is at all serious: one could say it's just a pact we agree: someone agrees to play someone else, and someone always agrees to play."

The girl stares at him: he picked up the white queen a long time ago and is holding her. He hugs her and puts her crown to his lips, what a big kiss . . . The man smiles and starts to set out the pieces, he likes to set them out neatly, in straight lines, facing each other, making it quite clear that the horses really would like to come out from behind the fence made by the pawns. The board is worn from so much use; it is made from the lids of the box that opens from the middle and inside is a piece of foam with spaces cut out where the pieces can be lodged. It is so worn the wood is shiny and looks metallic.

The girl is shivering. The park is flat and open and a light spring St Petersburg breeze is blowing and it is cold, too cold. It has just struck five o'clock and the trees are beginning to sieve the light. It is the end of April and the branches of trees and shrubs are beginning to sprout new green leaves that are soft and gentle and their white, translucent veins turn almost transparent, as if the tree tops were one huge stained glass window that tinges everything with an emerald glow. The sun is setting and flies and mosquitoes, even the odd butterfly or dragonfly, start to emerge from the edges of the pond in the middle of the park that the chess player's eyes pursue between the webs the spiders have spun from tree to tree, the finest threads that glisten and sway to the rhythm of the wind connecting the whole park.

The man has patiently set out the pieces, and it is a joy to see them. They are apparently awaiting their orders from the players hunched over the chessboard. The girl places her white queen in her square and, almost absent-mindedly, moves a pawn.

"Do you want to play? Do you really want to play?" the man asks, but the girl says nothing, simply smiles. "Oh, so you *do* want to play . . . Everyone wants to play, everyone wants to play, but I have to tell you that nothing comes free . . . If you lose, you must pay a forfeit, is that agreed? I will choose what it is later. You want to play then? The moment the first piece is moved, the game can't be stopped. Do you realise that? Do you accept the pact? Do you really want to play? They all think the game ends when it's all over, but a game is never over. As soon as it starts, the possibilities are infinite: a game is only one option taken from an in-finite range . . . Do you see? You can move a single pawn, but you could also let it be and make the horse jump over the fence, I told you there are lots of movements, and remember, then there is the other person's response, that can be unpredictable or necessary, you advance, I advance, both towards the middle of the board, to meet, it is inevitable, if we decide to play. Do you see, now you can swallow my pawn, I left it there for you, very good, you see? And now I will swallow you up. Oh, of course, many games have started like this, but just think how each movement we make means it is a new game, obviously there are the rules, I explained those, and the moves, but each game develops differently. Do you like it? I can see you do. I can see you want to play on. I will make it straightforward as it is your first game and I have been playing for many years. Do you see? Now you can kill my bishop, and that way we will get rid of a few pieces, the more we advance, the closer together our pieces, the closer together we are, the better . . ."

The sun has almost set; it has been cold for some time. The heat the afternoon brought to the park soon vanishes as the wind picks up. The light no longer shines beyond the tops of the trees and under the branches there is only the glare left by the long, steady twilight in this part of the world. The swans stretch their necks to reach crumbs a group of pensioners throw from the side, while a grandmother is picking the flowers from some bushes that lose all their petals as she pulls at them: spring twilights are the saddest. The nearby tables have been emptying out, there is only one game left now, a long way away, where two grandads are fighting over their few remaining pieces. It has got late.

They don't have many pieces left either. The man has advanced his horses as far as a line of pawns that straggles and boxes in the king and, in consequence, the queen. He has allowed almost all his pieces to be killed, he has only two horses, two black horses left that seem to be galloping wildly, she will soon have to surrender her queen. Checkmate is very close, two moves and it will be all over.

The girl looks at him and he has been staring into her eyes for some time. She is pretty, smooth-featured, with glinting hair and silvery laughter. Who knows where such a delicate thread might lead?

"Do you see, the white queen is mine, all mine, my horses have her cornered. I like playing with the horses, the horse is a clever animal, it is the only animal we have tamed that still frightens us, you are scared of horses, aren't you? You aren't? Very good. Horses are fascinating animals, they are a lot like men and that is why they scare us. What about centaurs? Do you know what a centaur is? Half man, half horse. Centaurs steal women and girls and take them into the woods on their hindquarters. But, of course, these are only stories, nothing real, just like chess, do you see? Look, checkmate and we are done."

The girl looks at him, it is almost dark under the trees now and the lights haven't been switched on yet, there are no blacks or whites, simply a mixture of shades of grey and murk, like the sky now beginning to be covered by a cold haze. The man has picked up the white queen and knocks the king over with one of his horses and the king rolls over the board until he hits the side of the box. The girl looks into his eyes, she now knows why nobody wants to play with him, she knows now.

Suddenly somebody starts shouting. A woman is walking round the side of the pond. "Love, love, love!" A tall woman, a jacket slung over her shoulders and holding another, a white one, against her heart. The woman walks this way and that, peering and shouting, "Love, love, love!" like a cat mewing to attract her kittens. She is well-dressed, was perhaps attractive once, now is just comely, and she walks along as if she is searching for someone. She finally waves an arm – "Love, love!" – and comes over to the table.

"Hey, love, where *have* you been? I've been looking for you for such a long time . . ."

"She's been here all the time, madam." The man gets up and shakes her hand. "Allow me to introduce myself, I am Vladimir. Your daughter sat down here and we have been playing chess."

The girl shakes his hand while her mother puts a jacket around her shoulders. The breeze has now turned into an unpleasant, blustery wind. The lamps have just been switched on, a cold, wan light that still can't blot out the glow of twilight.

"Oh, well, thank you. We must be going, it's late, you gave me such a fright, love, say goodbye to Mr Vladimir."

"We were playing, weren't we, my little pretty? I taught her how to play chess, she said she knew a little already and we played a game. She lost, but she will soon learn. She will be a good player."

The girl looks at him. She has never once stopped looking in all this time.

"I've not paid my forfeit," she says, still looking.

"Oh, yes you have! You paid, you spent the whole afternoon with me, we were finely entertained, you know, darkness even fell. We shall play another game, I'm sure we shall play another day."

"Say goodbye, say *au revoir* to Mr Vladimir."

"Goodbye, Mr Vladimir. Will we see each other again?"

"Yes, you can be sure we will. Goodbye, my little pretty."

The girl, who is gripping her mother's hand, turns around from time to time and looks backwards, catches another view of the man, who is looking in her direction as he turns the box round and slots the pieces into their allotted space. All except for the white queen that he grips tight in one hand. As the girl walks off, he rolls the queen's crown over his lips, the forfeit.

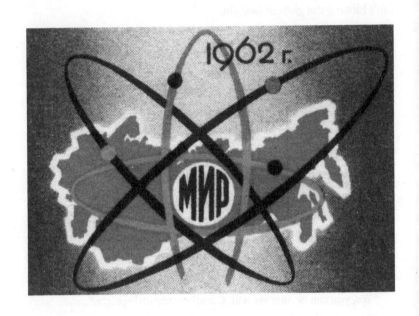

VERA-MARGARITA ABANSEREV

Vera-Margarita Abanserev (born Balashikha, 1949) has been as precocious, prolific and polemical as she is largely unpublished and, consequently, unknown. Her confrontations with the Party have brought constant, more or less acknowledged censorship and that has meant that some of her writing has disappeared. *Spiralling Journeys* was the work that brought her to the attention of the silent wider reading public. Readers appreciated her narrative daring and the virtues of a style and prose the author has said she will not repeat. The labours of the men who cut and reforest the virgin woods of the Urals are described with a precision that is quite unprecedented in Russian prose. The sense and meaning of some passages in the book have generated a fierce debate among academics, journalists, poets and critics. Some discern a defence of the utopia of a communism that becomes a path towards spirituality, and others, the need to flee a structure that frustrates the possibilities for the individual. *Stained Glass Without Light*, her first book of poetry, has been successfully republished by the Vosti publishing house. In terms of her major project, *Short History of a Country Without End*, we know that the author has allowed us to glimpse sparse fragments that confirm her great narrative talent. The following stories come from the book *Two Mammoths under the Ice*, winner of the prestigious Narodnaya Prize. The jury described the book as "the author's commitment to the history of individuals and the collective".

THE BALLAD OF RED SQUARE

They have seen him taking a stroll across the Dnieper marshes and also along the tracks that cut through the huge expanse of the taiga. They say they saw him walking along one of the paths that go across the steppes to the peaks of the Urals, even to the coldest, most inhospitable regions of Siberia. He had been seen standing silently before the Black, Caspian and Baltic Seas. Indeed, there are eyewitness accounts that swear he has visited the whole country, from east to west and north to south. Deserts and rivers could not stop him, nor the mudflats that hide the roads throughout the country in spring and autumn.

They also relate, however, that Moscow is where one can see him most often, the centre of Moscow, in Red Square. He roams here and there like a soul in limbo, perhaps that is what he is, a soul in limbo, a will o' the wisp now walking across the ice over the River Moscova, now halting opposite one of the gates of the Kremlin. He sometimes seems tired and sits down on one of the bollards that flank the entrance. They also say they have seen him meandering aimlessly, strolling by the side of Lenin's mausoleum, much to the astonishment of the guards, climbing up to the very spot from which Stalin and others reviewed endless army parades. Then, he sits down again in Lobnoye Mesto, the grandiose vision that seems to focus the gazes of all that cross the square. When he sits down, he does so like a grandfather, gradually, taking great care not to hurt himself, as if he were tired of so much restless wandering.

They recount that his longish, white hair is matted with his broad, thick beard. Yes, he has a keen eye, as in the photos. He sometimes carries a book that he pretends to read. Some seriously doubt the veracity of this apparition. It could all be, it might very well be, one of these myths people invent because they wish it were true, though it irks one to say so and to denigrate what people say, the stories they tell, with which they seem sometimes to be trying to hide what they can actually see in order to see something completely unreal.

Though that is not the case, no, it's not, because I saw him too. Only once, but I swear it *was* him. It was a freezing night and beginning to snow. Flakes were falling diagonally over the great square, driven by the north wind, but you could seem him clearly enough, sitting on the steps of Lobnoye Mesto. The esplanade was emptying out, as if the gusts were driving the crowds from the square, a huge white blanket spreading where only a few seconds ago pedestrians and tourists strolled or gaped. Not a sound, a snowy silence.

There was only one person in the whole square. An old woman who liked to doss down there, carrying a supermarket bag and wearing rags so ragged it was hard to distinguish the items of clothing from a series of remnants. A kind of apron hung down her body, plastic and wool patches sewn together down to her feet, like rough-and-ready leggings and, over her arms and shoulders, a long, tattered cloak made from miscellaneous rubbish attached to her head at one corner, a bag lady's raincoat. She chatted to herself and occasionally extracted a bottle from her tatters. She was drunk. She bawled, now sang a completely unintelligible song, now stopped and waved her arm as if she were conducting an orchestra. From time to time she slipped and then laughed, a cracked laugh that ended in a hoarse, doggish cough she choked on. The old woman then stretched out on all fours on the ground until she got her breath back. She moved very, very slowly, advancing through the snow as if she were trying to keep it at bay with her arms, until she fell down again. And that is how she dragged herself over the final few metres to the stairs, and pulled herself up the steps by her arms and legs until she was sitting next to him.

The old woman sang and every so often laughed, laughed so much she choked. Then coughed and coughed until she seemed to stop breathing, until she burst out laughing again. Only her head was visible. She had sat on the rubbish bag that covered almost the whole of her back and ended in a hood over her head. She laughed and laughed and laughed, and when she was out of breath started choking again. Then she muttered and took another swig and turned to the spectre and offered him the vodka. I could no longer see him, the snow was falling softly but so thickly it was hard to make out where you were, perhaps she alone could see him. Now and then the old woman wiped off the snow, the flakes that seemed intent on covering her. Indeed, in next to no time, the fresh snow hid even the footprints and trail that led to the stairs, and spread a spotless sheet over the square: everyone had gone home and she was alone in the square.

The old woman bawled and kept asking, "So, Father of the Fatherland, what am I supposed to do now? What am I supposed to do now?"

And she burst into more laughter until she choked, and the snow fell so slowly and thickly it looked like a curtain, a series of heavy folds above the stage. Snow was falling over the whole country, over the Dnieper marshes and the paths that go from the steppes to the Urals, falling on the tracks that traverse the taiga. Snow must be falling over every inhabitant of the country, on that night when the blizzards swirled over Siberia's treeless plains and blew over half the world until they finally melted on the savage, surging Baltic Sea, as if the same snowstorm was blanketing the whole country.

The snow continued well into the early morning, so much snow that it avalanched down from the top of every wall around the square and concealed every plinth. A thick layer of snow hid all the square's symbols, in White Square, and when it seemed the storm could bring no more snow, after the final gusts, when the wind blew itself out on those last strenuous efforts, the flakes began to thin out. Freezing air took command of Moscow and when the snow stopped the spectre walked up and down the square once again.

The old woman was stretched out on her rubbish sack on the ground, halfway up the stairs to Lobnoye Mesto, half whitened by the snow, as if she were sleeping.

It was a clear night, and the cold froze the substance of the air and made it transparent, transparent as vodka, like melting water and tears, like ice, cold, solid and transparent as that spectre, the ghost of Karl Marx, now sitting on the snow that covered the steps of Lobnoye Mesto and caressed the old woman's frozen locks.

Freezing ice transformed the square into one huge sheet of marble.

THE TRANSPARENCY OF EVIL

They couldn't hide their surprise at the checkpoints on the road: they were the first. They were the first to return. They checked and stamped their papers, and immediately let them pass. All in order.

The soldiers looked at them with a mixture of amazement and pity. They could understand there were people who had decided to stay but found it completely incomprehensible that others, once they had left, should come back. Pavla collected their papers and placed them back in the folder ready for the next checkpoint that would ask to see them. She started the engine and drove along the road that would take them as far as Tropnavitchi. Pavla was smiling, but for Guerassim and Marfa her grin was only a grimace that expressed resignation and unease.

They drove though the neighbouring town, Ipstavitchi, well into the night. The dim, flickering glow from the car headlights was all that lit up the abandoned streets and dark squares. Not a light was lit, not a single person, not even in the houses whose doors and windows were open, only a sudden spectacle of overgrown areas, grimy façades and streets full of potholes that Pavla tried to dodge.

The town was deserted; the whole district was deserted. The only company came from the distant, sporadic burst of light at each of the checkpoints. They were reminded of the hazy lights from years ago, from neighbouring villages and the paper factory and, above all, on the other side, from the power station.

Pavla glanced now and then in the rear-view mirror at her father's wrinkled, but tranquil face and her mother's deadpan expression. They had debated this step so often she knew nothing would change their minds, and she didn't want to start another argument before she returned them to their home. She had got used to the idea, but even so, she was still hoping for a miracle, something that would prevent them from staying, a blocked road, a fire, whatever obstacle might stop their progress and force them to retreat, but everything stayed the same, no change, as ever. At most it was slightly more sombre, or sadder.

Her father's legs gripped the bag that reached down to his feet. Her mother tried to make herself comfortable in the back seat, grappling with the bags and parcels falling on her skirt and feet at every pothole and bump; the car was loaded down with clothes, provisions and kitchenware, soap. They had been warned that everything in their house was contaminated. As well as the house itself. And the land, and the water from the wells, but that was different, they could change nothing there. And the air, the air coming through the vents of the heater and warming them, Pavla reflected, and the air they were breathing, even the car was . . . She had already decided to sell it once that trip was over and buy a new one. She would have to throw away her clothes and shoes. And cut her hair really short. In theory, none of that was necessary; in practice . . .

They reached Tropnavitchi at last, the neighbouring village that Pavla drove through until she found the turning that led to her parents' house. She manoeuvred at the end of the track, parked near the front door and switched off the engine. Guerassim Lebedev, her father, and her mother, Marfa Yefimovna, were smiling, it was almost midnight, but both were smiling.

"We're home, love, we're back home," they said.

Yes, they were home. Pavla helped her mother to get out of the car, immediately slipped on gloves, took a torch and went down to the cellar. The generator's motor jerked into action and lit up the lights in the passage and out in the garden. It was all as they had left it, covered in dust, of course, but no-one had touched anything. Marfa was laughing and kept repeating that it was all as was, nobody had touched a thing, it was all as was. Who *was* ever going to touch a thing? Soldiers were everywhere and everything was contaminated, who would ever go there to steal? As soon as she emerged from the cellar, Pavla threw all the windows open and then, after she had turned on the water, she started the flow from the taps, the shower, the sink, the lavatory, the kitchen and washhouse taps, a stream of rusty water that gradually cleared. Those were the minimal precautions she had read that one should take, let the contaminated water flow through the pipes until fresh water – that would be less contaminated – filled the system.

In the meantime, her father and mother had emptied the car. Rows of parcels lined the passage and their clothes were on the dining-room table. Marfa wiped the kitchen surfaces with a wet cloth and set down the cans of vegetables, pots of jam and bags of bread. Pavla went into the garage and tried to start her father's car, but had to open up the engine, it had been out of action for so long. She finally drove it out of the garage and left it outside with the engine running: it spluttered and juddered to a halt.

"You get going, Pavla," her father told her, "we're back now, the shorter your stay the better, your mother and I will sort ourselves out, we've got water and light and the car's still working. We've got all we need, love, we're worried for your sake, the shorter your stay the better."

But Pavla was still finding things to do, the basic precautions, she was worried they might forget the odd one. Windows and taps were still open, and the car was still running, charging the battery. She started to remove clothes from the wardrobes and organise them into piles. As soon as she had emptied the lot, she took it all out into the garden and

67

made a big bonfire. And not a single cross word from her father or mother, it was the agreement they had made to allow them to return, to get rid of everything that wasn't vital and take the basic precautions . . . But not their hats, shoes and boots – that was what they had agreed. Her father owned lots of hats, which he really cherished, and the boots were too expensive.

"Come on, Pavla, you go home. We're back and we're fine and nothing's going to happen to us, we've got the list of things we must do and I promise you we will."

"Father, I'm alright, you're back home, you know I asked you . . ."

"We've talked too much. Far too much, Pavla," her mother replied from the kitchen, "we've got the list and will do the lot, now you start off home, you're making us suffer. And don't give this another thought, love, we'll be alright."

"At least let me wash down the house."

"Your father can do that. You go home, Pavla, go home, you're making us suffer. We're here now, we'll sort ourselves out, everything works, everything is fine." Marfa was worried, she knew nothing was going to happen to her, but even so she was frightened.

"I don't know if I can, Mother, I should snatch a couple of hours, sleep, to get over all the stress, I really should. I'll stretch out on the back seat."

"Love . . ."

"No, Mother, I'd fall asleep on the road. We took longer to reach here than I anticipated, what with the checkpoints. Don't worry, I can just stretch out on the back seat."

Pavla spread one of the blankets she took out of a bag of bed linen across the back seats, removed her shoes and lay down. Guerassim knocked on the window and said goodnight. Marfa opened the door.

"Pavla, please go, don't sleep here, go to the hotel."

"No, Mother, that would be too many hours on the road, don't you understand what a long haul it was to get here? I'm sure it's a good two hours to a hotel in a safe zone and then it will probably be full. Don't worry, it's only till the morning, just a few hours, I'll be alright."

Marfa didn't answer, simply said goodnight and went into her home to sleep next to Guerassim. They left the house, door and windows open and when the bedroom light went out, the generator's automatic switch clicked and the motor stopped dead. There was complete silence. Chernobyl and its radiation kept the whole area quiet, night and day.

The quiet lasted more than six hours, until the sun woke her up. She had enjoyed a good rest and although the windows were steamed up and covered in dew, she hadn't felt cold or damp. She got out of the car without making a sound and went in search of a demijohn of water to have a wash. She went deep into the woods to go to the lavatory and then walked back to the house. Marfa and Guerassim were still asleep, exhausted: they weren't used to going on such long journeys. Pavla made herself a sandwich and ate gherkins and cheese. It had all happened so quickly she'd not had time to see how pretty the place was with the sun rising above the mist. We've forgotten what life is about, she thought as she watched the mists float beneath the sun.

She went up to the upstairs bedroom and sat down on the side of the bed.

"We'll get up soon, love, we'll soon be up," Marfa told her.

"Mother, we can put everything back in the car in a matter of minutes and drive back home, easy as pie. We really can."

"Love, home is here, our home is here, we've been through that. Don't start again. We'll come to visit. You can see the house is alright, so is the car, everything, you can't see a thing wrong, love, we'll be fine, nothing's going to upset us. Come on, have you had breakfast? We'll be down in a moment to say goodbye."

"Mother . . ."

"That's enough of that, my little Pavla, it's fine here, you can't see a thing, come on, don't start all over again, you must be going and I want to say goodbye in a spirit of peace," she said, sitting up in bed. Guerassim was just waking up.

True, you couldn't see a thing. In fact, no-one ever had seen a thing, and whatever you did manage to see it was better not to see at all. You couldn't see a thing, and that was what she felt was most disturbing, not seeing a thing, the monster that deformed men had no form, no substance, no weight, wasn't even air, and was nowhere to be seen. That was what most disturbed her, that the beast surrounding them was nowhere yet everywhere, was like the Devil, she'd heard her mother say, if God could be everywhere, so could the Devil, if everything could be full of God, everything could equally be full of the Devil. Good had no form, neither did evil, she'd once heard an old lady remark.

They had never seen much at all, not even at the time when the accident happened, only a plume of smoke rising out of the power station. Television drip-fed images very slowly. Maps and more maps with concentric circles, and even more maps indicating which way the wind was blowing. The nuclear power station burned as if it were a humble carpenter's shop. Technology, worldwide power . . . all the energy of the Union escaped through that hole, as if it were a balloon that had burst. As if it were a huge vessel that was gradually sinking down into the waters of the world, the hole at the Plimsoll line simply indicating we were aboard a river barge and not a battleship that could harbour in any port of the future without fearing what fate held in store, as the power-station loudspeakers had proclaimed the day it was inaugurated.

Chernobyl was burning, and the television news only showed clouds of stupid smoke and poor wretches throwing earth and rocks inside the hole and cement, lots of cement – quick, fill it in, run to it, everybody –

and there was nothing to show, because the worst couldn't be broadcast, it was impossible, no way you could record what was happening, because it was all invisible, the radiation didn't exist, it would cause thyroid cancer and malformations and throat cancer and would make the earth unusable, contaminate it, but the air was as transparent as ever. But all the same, you could see nothing, could see nothing of any of that.

There were hardly any photos, a very few that were very bad. Like a comic strip, drawings enlightened most, drawings of the inside of the power station, figures representing the processing of materials, graphs illustrating energy production and most terrible of all, the spreading of an evil that no-one could see. The air smelled the same as always, so did water and bread, and the trees weren't disfigured in any way, but on that occasion it was no simulation, it wasn't one of the many test checks they had carried out in the towns all around, the alarms didn't stop ringing and the lorries that at other times had brought make-believe drama now came in deadly earnest. The soldiers refused to let anyone leave the town and even knocked on Marfa and Guerassim's door. They couldn't go out and weren't allowed to drink the water, or shower with the water from their tanks, the soldiers would bring them drinking water and food, for three days.

In the end they were evacuated, like everybody else, evacuated because they lived too close to the power station, and some were transported to Minsk and others to Kiev and to other towns and cities, thousands of displaced people in flight from an invisible enemy, who was nowhere to be seen, only the effects were visible. But everybody knew what they were talking about: nobody knew exactly how radiation worked, but everybody was aware of how it might affect them.

And it was strange, because there were no signs of storm damage. It was about invisible effects, as if the invisibility of the causes infected the consequences as well. The house was intact, just slightly dustier, like the land, like the road, with just slightly overgrown weeds revealing that the area had been abandoned, next to nothing really, the place seemed almost intact. But they *were* being pursued by something that was formless, times a-changing over Russia, as if the matter from which the matter derives was in revolt and bent on self-destruction, that's why, they were informed, boys and girls might be born malformed, and that anyone who had been overexposed to this change might contract incurable illnesses. Things were disintegrating from within.

It was cold. Pavla took a jersey out of the car boot; she hadn't left anything outside. She switched on the ignition and left the car warming up while Marfa and Guerassim came to the front door. They hugged tight, as people do when they haven't seen each other for a long time or when they know it will be a very long time before they meet again. They kissed and wiped away some tears.

"If anything happens, ring me and I'll come at once."

"Don't you fret, little Pavla, we'll call you from the soldiers' check-point, we'll write to each other and we'll come to visit, go in peace, daughter."

Pavla drove down the road out of town. By day, Tropnavitchi and the town seemed even sadder, like dogs that had been abandoned, that were filthy, with matted manes and hair, with the weeds growing on roofs and the cracks in the road. Pavla was moving away from the concentric circles that marked out the exclusion areas and she was thinking back to the day when she had finally been able to see Marfa and Guerassim and bring them to her house. She had a spare room and they were comfortable there. They were unable to find out precisely what was happening around Chernobyl until they read the foreign press and saw the photographs and even the videos that were circulating clan-destinely. Guerassim and Marfa reached Oriol with not much more than they had been given by the authorities, a bag with soap and flannels and the little they had been able to take from home, the odd piece of clothing, their papers and Marfa's earrings. Like so many other displaced people, they spent more than two years away from home, in temporary accommodation, in the homes of relatives or children, monitoring the situation as it developed. In Pavla's house they experienced that situation with a kind of subdued normality, but normality nevertheless, the same resignation with which they could have faced compulsory displacement and changes of address or work.

And it continued like that up to the day when they discovered there were people who had refused to leave, elderly folk like themselves who had decided to stay put. Then the six months of push and pull started, of perhaps we should go back, of days that brought the latest news, of the fact that some people did stay put . . . Pavla refused to countenance any of that, a single word about returning home, after all that had happened . . . During all those months she had continually thought of their house, had scrutinised the maps and pinpointed it inside one of the circles that had been drawn around the power station, those she now crossed as she drove back to her home in Oriol.

While Pavla was returning home, Guerassim was washing his down and itching to go for a walk, but Marfa had told him that first they must wash out the house as they had promised little Pavla. As well as their car. Marfa had shut all the windows and Guerassim had switched on the water pump and began to wash down the roof, time and again, and then the façade, the side-walls and the shutters and the windows, spending the whole morning on that while Marfa mopped the floor inside with buckets of water. As soon as he had washed down the façade, Guerassim fastened down the hose and let it wash the roof and other parts, as if it were raining. They removed the curtains and everything that wasn't indispensable, everything that was more or less contaminated, though

73

they wouldn't have bothered if they hadn't promised Pavla that they would.

Now and then Guerassim asked, "This too?" and then Marfa, almost without looking up, said yes, that too should be burned, and continued with her mopping.

Ah, they were finally back home! And true enough, outside, next to their garden the curtains and two settees were burning on top of the embers of yesterday's bonfire, and now they must paint the walls and wash down the house again. But it was also true that they had brought healthy seeds with them. They would replant their garden! They would remove the topsoil, the most contaminated earth, and grow vegetables once again! They were well aware they would be contaminated in the end, they had been in contact with their tools, by dint of touching the hose and washing the house down, mopping the floor, by dint of coming back and breathing the air they breathed inside their home.

But so what? Guerassim was sixty-nine and Marfa would soon be sixty-seven, they might perhaps make it to eighty, but both doubted they would, they had worked too hard. "We're worked out, Pavlina," they finally argued when all their other arguments went nowhere, "we're worked out, we'll never make it to eighty." They remembered seeing her tears, and more than once, but the conviction that they must return home finally won out.

"The house is intact, nothing had changed, love, nothing at all," they repeated as soon as they arrived, as if they had to convince her of something. They couldn't detect any difference, and thought that, at the end of the day, it would be easier to adapt to tragedy if that tragedy were completely invisible. And though it was forbidden, they would plant their vegetables and would breed poultry and rabbits again, and bake bread, would buy flour in the city . . . They weren't bothered about being alone in town, they had been the first to return, and no-one had stayed behind in Tropnavitchi. They knew some grandmas and grandads had stayed on in neighbouring towns. They thought they might pay them a visit; they'd be sure to be pleased to have someone else to talk to.

While Pavla returned to her work and resumed her daily routines after more than three days on the road, Guerassim and Marfa finished their cleaning.

In less than a fortnight they had burned most of the things they couldn't wash, had washed down the house dozens of times and even prepared the land to replant their garden. They went out for a stroll before it got dark and went to bed the moment they could see nothing. They lived by the sun in order to save on diesel fuel. The soldiers treated them well, let them make calls, brought them the parcels Pavla sent from the city to the checkpoint and even once gave them oil from their tank, produced a pipe, sucked out the fuel and filled the demijohns that Guerassim brought up from the cellar. They laughed and joked and asked them for their daughter's telephone number.

Pavla sent them a parcel every week, cold sausage, tinned meat and powdered milk, canned fruit, a little sugar and soap, anything she thought they might need. She had sold her car and thrown out all the clothes she'd been wearing the day she drove them home, everything was gradually returning to normal, she had even started to think they would be happier in their own home and not in the city, they had lived their whole lives there. Guerassim and Marfa had worked in the paper-making factories in the area from early on. They had met at work and worked there until they retired, with the single exception, naturally, of the Great Patriotic War. But as soon as the factory was rebuilt, Guerassim and Marfa returned to their spindles and guillotines and the pulp, back to their daily toil. Then Pavla came, the great joy of their lives, and then one by one those great events of history passing unnoticed through their little town. Guerassim and Marfa made paper, abided by

75

the hours and the production levels demanded, by everything that was expected of them, they kept their side of the bargain and trusted that everything would go as they were told it would go, well, everything would run like clockwork, with an order and predictability that were perfectly planned.

Marfa and Guerassim's lives were tranquil once again, like the calm after the storm, with hours aplenty and tranquil days that were only interrupted by the weekly calls from their Pavlina. They had to go to the soldiers' checkpoint and wait until it was time and, if they were talking on the phone, they would have to wait until little Pavla got a line. The soldiers laughed and asked if they could have a word too. They also laughed. How peaceful it was to stroll along paths where no-one now strolled, that grew wilder by the day, where the trees stood so proud. The landscape, without people, was magnificent. They strolled by the side of canals and marshes, through meadows where nothing now grew, everywhere, without a soul to bother them, there was never anyone, only the soldiers' checkpoints, soldiers who no longer asked to see their papers.

Once they even walked close to the power station. The roads were a mess, destroyed by the wheels of caterpillars, tractors and jeeps. All around they saw tanks and reinforced concrete pillars, scrap iron from the towers, like the remains of a shipwreck. From a distance, the shape of the power station reminded them of a vessel marooned in the void. Like the radiation: at once nothing and everything. The whole district was abandoned. They were like two survivors of a shipwreck, the last to survive the debacle.

When they arrived home, they switched on their generator, had dinner, and when they turned off their bedroom light all was silent.

FACING THE ARAL SEA

The sentence attributed to Lenin, "Trust is all very well, but control is even better", was first uttered in public in a speech in Moscow by Andrei Fiodorovitch Rauschs, better known as Sirdarin, now unheard of and forgotten. Sirdarin was one of the many heads the Party-monster kept devouring. Other less renowned one-liners of his include "In a democracy one must serve the voter, in a dictatorship as well" and "No cold, no communism". By "voter" he meant the person who appointed the chief of police, civil servant or manager, not the citizenry; by "cold", Siberia.

That's all buzzing around my head today after visiting the city where Andrei Fiodorovitch Rauschs was born, near the Aral Sea, that at the present moment is a parched expanse with vessels anchored in a barren plain that had previously been the bottom of a fresh-water sea. Sirdarin didn't enter history. Indeed, history passed him by: almost no trace of his existence remains. No point in regretting that, however, he is hardly worth the bother.

The arguments one does find in the annals are those between Lenin and Volgin. There have even been angry debates about who first decided to choose the names of rivers, but all quite mistaken. Sirdarin got there first: you cannot deny that he was quite brilliant when it came to one-liners or selecting names, perhaps if he had stuck to that his career wouldn't have been so abruptly curtailed: if only he had occasionally listened to or read himself! Andrei Fiodorovitch Rauschs was the first to use the name of a river as a pseudonym, Sirdarin, the last heir to a family of merchants in decline, from generation after generation of Austrians who were almost bourgeois but never quite made the grade. In fact, the one-liner "Trust is all very well, but control is even better" isn't his, it is a German saying his father repeated from time to time when he was checking the precise weight of sacks of whatever he happened to be buying or when he was reproaching Andrei Fiodorivitch in that harsh, impassive tone of his for the dilatory way he kept the accounts of the business or watched over their shop assistants.

Andrei Fiodorovitch will not then enter history on any account. If it hasn't happened, it never will, and this short note won't be the lever to make it happen. His one-liners are not without wit: "Implanting communism in Russia is as difficult as trying to make a to-scale map of the place"; "God is great, but Russia is even greater". And his skill in choosing nicknames was also renowned: he sentenced a toothless, breathless leader to carry forever the nickname of Walrus. He gave Lenin the idea of choosing the Lena or Volgin; Georgei Valentinovitch Plekhanov decided on the Volga before Lenin. Sirdarin had chosen the Syrdarj that he had watched in full flood as a child.

We know he had several meetings with Lenin, that he met Trotsky and a youthful Khrushchev. Trotsky famously said of him: "Sirdarin is as dispensable as he is irritating." A sentence that was applied to Trotsky himself after the purges had seen to Andrei Fiodorovitch.

Sirdarin noticed he seemed to be in the way at a lunch with other Party leaders. They all sat in their places except for him: he'd not been allocated a chair. Despite his complaints nobody managed to find a chair in the entire building. When one did finally arrive from the other side of the road, his soup was cold. Sirdarin couldn't identify the voice that bawled, "No cold, no communism!"

Within a few months Andrei Fiodorovitch became just another victim of the purges and the River Syrdarj has now been drained, dammed and bled so much the sea it once fed was reduced to naught. Trusting in the river was all very well, but controlling it, some might say, was even better.

GUILT

If the mirror is broken, don't use it to see yourself
BORIS SLAVINSKI, a woodcutter from Byelorussia

They would meet again! Twenty-two years later! After twenty-two wintry years, they would meet again!

They too had finally received the official permit rescinding all previous sanctions. They had been informed of the notices lifting the bans and it was confirmed that even though they wouldn't be restored to their previous places of work, they would recover their salary level and the right to return to the body for which they worked. They had the same freedom of movement as other citizens, were no longer spied on, could change their place of residence and seek permission to purchase a house or a car. By the end of two months everyone had been notified. Aleksei and Maria Bulgariov couldn't believe it, after twenty-two years.

The Izmailovs were the first. Before they let the others know, they made sure it wasn't a mistake or trap, anything being possible. But it was all in order and, moreover, they were informed that all their colleagues would very soon be hearing since it wasn't the review of a single case, but the whole slate wiped clean. They were exonerated and asked to forgive the delays.

The Izmailovs rang the Orembergs.

"Oleg, Oleg, we've received the letter," said Ivan and Aleksandra Izmailov, both glued to the phone, "we have received the letter, you will receive one shortly, very shortly, the whole case has been annulled!"

And the Orembergs rang Mikhail.

"Mikhail, Mikhail, the Izmailovs have received the letter, we're sure you will receive yours soon, it's just a matter of time, Mikhail, we so want to see you, we love you so much, Mikhail. As soon as we have the letter we'll come to Omsk. We'll book a call from the exchange."

"Yes," said Mikhail, "I really want to see you too, Marina."

The news leapt from home to home as everyone phoned each other. It wasn't enough to tell one's nearest and dearest, it was so cheering to spread the joy to every member of the group. Mikhail was the first person the Orembergs rang.

Mikhail didn't want to spin out the conversation, and one had to be careful with Mikhail: after Vilma died (who drank a lot – too much) they had heard he had been interned twice. They always read Mikhail's letters with great sadness, they were sent with tears and read with tears. He wasn't the only one: the Trubetskayas and the Volkonskis couldn't handle it and divorced, then Aleksandr hung himself.

Aleksandr's death impacted on the whole group and nothing was the same from that day on. Ever since Aleksandr's death they, the Bulgariovs, and all their closest friends, the Orembergs, the Galernayas and the Hevalskis, had organised a small nucleus that fought to keep them all united and stiffen their resolve. They were the ones who felt they had more energy to bolster the others. After the first three years, they realised from the letters they were receiving that the new situation had sunk in.

The mail was the only form of communication allowed. That was why they decided to use the letters to keep their spirits up; that was why they kept writing endlessly, though they knew their letters were being opened. Initially, it was through third parties, friends in the factory they trusted sufficiently for them to send their letters to the friends of their friends. When they stopped interfering with their correspondence, the number of letters multiplied, it was all about getting their letters out to the others, come what may, as many as possible, so the others were compelled to reply. They sometimes wrote about their newly born children, sometimes about the changes in their respective factories, sometimes about the books they were in the middle of reading. Twenty-two years . . . They took care not to describe their joys in too much detail to those experiencing bad times; each letter was a balancing act between what they could say, what they wanted to say and what they had to say. They had boxes and drawers full of letters, hundreds and thousands: they could only allow themselves one call a month. After twenty-two years they could now forget the letters and meet every day.

They, Maria and Aleksei Bulgariov, together with the Orembergs, the Galernayas and the Hevalskis, had been the most active group and had struggled to sustain it from the moment the trial ended. From time to time, they would hint in a letter that they had sprained their wrists from so much writing. They coordinated the whole correspondence and ensured that Mikhail always received his weekly letter, and that the Volkonskis and Maria Trubetskaya always received a food and clothes parcel.

They were the luckiest, and once even managed to meet up with the Hevalskis at an assembly of workers from different factories. They had been located in relatively close cities and believed that the fact they could spend a whole day together talking face to face about what they had been doing all that time was down to a planning error. And perhaps they had already explained all that by letter, but now they could see how both sides argued, hear each other's voices, and though it was only seven or eight hours that simply flew by, both couples remembered that time as if it had been a dream they wouldn't have changed for all the gold in the world. They met their respective children and hugged, Marina and Irina clinging together like a couple of girls in the playground. The moment they separated they started hugging again. They held hands even when they had to go and listen to the speeches.

They lived on that chance encounter for a year, aware that it was the most important event in their lives and no doubt would remain so for a long, long time. Nevertheless, they only told the companions who seemed relatively resilient, spirited and settled. The slightest thing could rock the others, given they had so much time on their hands to think, and who knows what conclusions they might draw. If they discovered the others had been able to meet up, who could say what they might have concluded. It was a constant struggle to ensure that upsets and the passage of time didn't rupture the group, despite it having been split up and scattered around the whole territory of the Union, and didn't rupture the bonds that kept their hopes alive. The Orembergs, Galernayas and Hevalskis had decided on that after a year of sending and receiving letters through third parties, and their decision led to a whole raft of correspondence with the others, twenty-five cells Irina had marked out on the map of the Union that hung on their dining-room wall. They had hung it there when they realised that they had stopped searching their flat when they went out to work. Up to that point they had kept their letters and all their other papers in a hiding-place in the factory.

They had all received the same letter, they were lifting all the sanctions and bans, previous work status would be restored and, even though they weren't returning the roubles that had been confiscated, everyone now had a right to a home in the cities where they formerly resided. They all returned to Kiev, to "the City", as they dubbed it.

They did so with the utmost caution: they all secured transport so they would reach the City at the same time. They even collected money to send to the Volkonskis and Maria Trubetskaya. They, Marina and Oleg Oremberg, were the first to arrive. All they could do on their first two days was stroll from one end of the City to the other and back. It was summer and very hot, Nikolka and Larissik, their children, couldn't believe their eyes, they were walking in the city they had heard so much about and didn't have to think about returning to Omsk in the morning. Marina and Oleg took charge of finding a place where they could meet. They were finally granted a refectory in the university and would thus meet in the same place where they had met twenty-two years ago. Some teachers were still around from that time and they helped them talk to the new administrators.

For the first time, Marina and Oleg revisited the corridors of the university, the lecture theatres, the lavatories, the doors to their old offices . . . They had often thought of that moment, what they would do, how they would feel as they walked back in, even though it was only to arrange tables and prepare food for their friends. They were almost more afraid of their reunion with the teachers they shared classes with than with their friends from the time when they used to organise meetings, but fortunately the pace of events didn't allow them to wallow in worry, fortunately it was summer and almost everyone at the university was on holiday. Only a couple of acquaintances from "their previous life", as they called it, were around.

The police must have listened to them from close by, in the other wing, the old wing of the university – they still didn't know why they were spied on or why they were deported. And it wasn't that they were unaware it might happen, they had heard about the horrible things that had taken place! But they remained uncertain about the real reasons that led them to be removed from their posts and scattered throughout the Union.

They didn't know why and possibly never would. There could be so many motives that perhaps even they would never be able to distinguish what was true from the whole entangled mess of revelations and betrayals. The number of motives was potentially so high they had been unable to identify a single reason to spark so many. It could be attributed to almost anything, awareness of similar cases led them to that conclusion: anything from other professors' envy to a simple need to meet the quotas for arrests, from possible internal strife in the local Party branch to the wish to inflict damage on particular members of the group, and all those other things that had tortured them for so many, many years.

One day a letter was delivered to their homes that accused them of plotting against the Union, of sedition, of being against the Party of the Republic. The whole group was accused and they were lucky: they had been betrayed by an outsider. Separate trials were staged and nobody knew what questions the others were being asked or whether the others were receiving any kind of reprieve for informing on them. They still couldn't understand how they hadn't been driven crazy, because they were being accused of sedition when all they had done was read and recite texts by Tolstoy and Blok and discuss them with a group of students. Obviously, they had also read Bulgakov, and many other writers who were frowned upon. The charges kept piling up, every single one quite improbable, but they were powerless, because the more they tried to prove they had done nothing against the norm, the worse their case became. They were reminded of the case of that madwoman, the woman awarded a medal for her services because she had denounced so many. And she continued her denunciations until they realised she was crazy. Hundreds of people were interrogated and imprisoned because of one round of informing by a lunatic woman. As far as their case was concerned, there were men and women in the group who broke down and said it was true that they had done bad things, but they never said what exactly, they had read books aloud, and in the presence of students, but which books? And more and more books began to surface, banned books, foreign books, books they shouldn't have circulated, books that . . . They had known right from the start that the moment the legal machinery whirred into action it would be totally impossible to put the brakes on it.

And then an enormously long trial from which they expected some kind of sentence or judgment. They knew, on the advice of lawyer friends, that they wouldn't be imprisoned and that they wouldn't be sentenced to forced labour, the most likely scenario was that they would be dispersed throughout the country and given an inferior labour status, that they would be put to work in a factory. With the passage of time they all realised the trial had been the worst of it, that and the fact that they had been sentenced for no reason at all, perhaps as the result of suspicion or betrayal.

The trial was what really hurt. As soon as they received their sentences, the huge number of changes in their lives meant they had no time to think about how all those shifts and dislocations were part of the punishment. Marina and Oleg decided to think that it was like a change of job, that the fact they had been sent to Novossibirsk *was* down to a change of job, it was better to think that, the sooner they got used to seeing it like that, the better.

And now, while Marina was setting out the serviettes and paper plates on the tables in the meeting room, Oleg was dragging stacks of chairs. Larissik and Nikolka had arranged an excursion to the City with the children of their parents' other colleagues. Everything was almost ready, they had the bottles, the soup saucepan and the trays with the meat inside a warm room, the bottles were on ice, and Marina was already laying out the cutlery that had been provided by the university canteen, and the glasses and the dishes of gherkins and beetroot. They began to hear voices and footsteps in the corridor, drawing nearer and nearer, rather sooner than they had anticipated, before they had put all the chairs in place.

Marina and Oleg often spoke about that moment, when they saw everybody walk in, when they saw them come in and stand on the other side of the table. Oleg wasn't ready for that, he was almost sick, the words wouldn't come, until he rested on the table. And then, everyone hugging everyone, and tears and shouts, even people who couldn't stop crying or who hugged until it seemed that they could never be separated, still wearing their overcoats, their bags on the floor, all together once again, at last.

They couldn't even eat lunch, everyone said it was just as well they had soup for a first course, because they had such lumps in their throats they would never have swallowed anything else. They gossiped and gossiped, and gossiped even more, they all brought something to the table, women produced cakes and desserts from their bags, savoury pastries, flaky pastries, all sorts. By the end they even laughed when they recalled the times when they were young, before the trials, the anecdotes about their reading group that were still very vivid, the day they staged Pushkin's *Mozart and Salieri* or read Lermontov's poetry and the lights went out and they continued in the dark, in candlelight, or even more strikingly, when they travelled to Poltava and the bus was caught in a blizzard and they had to spend the night on the road and sleep huddled next to each other, including the driver who left the engine running to keep the heating going, and someone had to be on duty to rev up the engine, and how they laughed, how the women pissed from the steps of the bus and then threw snowballs on their piss, and how they laughed and laughed. And occasionally burst into tears, but they avoided talking about what they all must have suffered, and kept talking about those times, because they only wanted to remember the years before the trials.

Marina and Oleg often spoke about it, how the long lunch was but an accompaniment to welcoming their colleagues' entry into the room, that Oleg remembers perfectly how he was sick, and that when he saw them coming in, the first thing that flashed up were the twenty-two years that had gone by since they were dispersed throughout the country. How wretched! Oleg must have thought, and that same second he realised the others must have felt exactly the same when they saw them. My God, twenty-two years have gone by.

They often spoke about that: about how when they walked in the Tasznavurians were there, who after working in the cultural department of a news agency ended up in a fish factory. About how they sent Maria Trubetskaya to Magadan, where she had a truly miserable time, isolated at the other end of the Union, living in dreadful conditions, where a voice was no use at all, where it had been ruined in the factory cold stores, and though she kept rehearsing every day, that's right, every day, her voice dried up, lost its life day by day, and, in fact, when she was talking, you heard the gentle tone and regulated breathing of a singing teacher, but also a strong nasal sound, no doubt caused by the continuous low temperatures in the cold stores. And she wasn't the only one whose voice had changed, Sergei Bolzsberg's had as well, he had ended up in a sawmill, and spent the whole day shouting in order to move the logs that kept coming at him backwards or forwards.

Tatiana Bolzsberg had lost part of one hand. The Bolzsbergs were forced to move close to the Kuibishev dams. Boris and Dusya Jurbarkas had been sent to the Voronezh potato and sugar beet fields, and the Arsakovs to a paper mill in Gomel, in Byelorussia, they were the ones nearest to the City, they were the ones who had been luckiest, and had even returned secretly once, in the final years of their banishment. The

Boltanskis had drawn the short straw, iron-ore mines on the Kola Peninsula. He was quite worn out and in pain when he breathed, even Anna lost her temper when he tried to light a cigarette.

Their luck was uneven. If they had got a foundry in Novossibirsk and the Glazovs a collective farm two hundred kilometres from Vologda, some people had been forced to go and work in the Komi gas refineries. What's more, if they, the Hevalskis, the Galernayas and the Orembergs had been able to exorcise their fears in a more or less tolerable manner, without fear of more repression stopping them from living their lives, the rest had experienced unending toil and trouble. Like Efim Liskevitch, the Volkonskis and so many others they didn't know about, and Mikhail, who had to drink himself silly every day, who drank non-stop. Mikhail who was no longer a doctor but a worker on a car production line. Aleksandr had hung himself, and his widow, Maria Trubetskaya, still hadn't got over it.

And when they saw everybody, but everybody, inside that room, on the other side of the table, they simply saw the history of the Union, saw those faces, the wasted years, the decades wasted by betrayal and absurdity. They thought how the sentences had marked them all, had disfigured and belittled them, the sentences had forced them to experience what the country was living through, that and that alone, men and women separated or united by force, compelled to be mere pins on a map, isolated from each other, reduced to nought.

ЧТО
ТЫ СДЕЛАЛ
ДЛЯ ВОЗДУШНОГО ФЛОТА?

VITALI KROPTKIN

Vitali Kroptkin (Elista, 1932 – Baku, 1997) is renowned for his articles and reporting on countries in the orbit of Soviet influence. The chronicles of his journeys to Cuba, Angola, Mongolia or the Yemen, with the pseudonym Viktor Sebastopol for a by-line, were read eagerly by thousands of readers who found that their irony opened a window on worlds that were so different and yet so similar to the world of Soviet Russia at the beginning of the 1960s. His wife figured in his chronicles and was the thread linking and contrasting them with the Russia Kroptkin said he carried within himself. She was blinded in Cambodia after an accident that left him with a permanent limp. The stories we are introducing first appeared in the centre-pages of the magazine *Horizon*, published by the Foreign Ministry's Directorate of International Relations. Dmitri Kriabin, the editor, described Kroptkin as a master in the art of loosening the rope the powers-that-be of the time were continually tightening. For five years Kroptkin read his articles and dramatised his stories on Radio Baku. His only work of fiction, *Perennial Flower: The Life without Works of Mikhail K.*, is a novel that tells of the difficulties of understanding otherness. The protagonist, a Mongol, the son of an Englishman who travelled to Asia, is finally chosen to represent his district before the Mongolian government and to mediate with the Russians who lived near the frontier. Kroptkin committed suicide the day after his wife died.

ELVIS PRESLEY SINGS IN RED SQUARE

In the most faraway box of every archive the K.G.B. hid, is hiding and ever will hide, lies the most carefully concealed document of any prepared in the President's Office. And it isn't a map of armament locations, or even of the largest untapped oil and gas fields, and, of course, it isn't a guide to the underground bunkers where the leaders of the U.S.S.R. would scurry in the event of a nuclear crisis, because that is hardly a great secret . . . In my capacity as the writer of the final section I was able to read the entire thing and have lived to tell the tale because the special nature of the event meant both sides insisted on one condition: that all involved should be allowed to survive.

The daily report of sessions in the Kremlin from a day one November describes one of the most absurd incidents in what we refer to as the Cold War. Oh, that Cold War, so much ado about so very little!

Indeed, these documents must also be lodged in the most subterranean of subterranean vaults in the Pentagon, and it is most likely that they will be destroyed when all such documents are destroyed that vanish before they are declassified.

Consequently, if it weren't for this confession of mine, nobody would know that Elvis Presley gave a concert in Moscow's Red Square.

Yes, you heard me, a concert in Red Square in 1958.

It was one of the many demonstrations of strength the superpowers made during the Cold War. A stupid one, but it was, at the end of the day, a demonstration of strength. An act of folly defined by a Russian

93

leader as a great act of love between Mother Russia and the American people. As time has gone by, some commentators have tried to read into that leader's words a first metaphor for *perestroika*: Elvis in Red Square sowed the wild oats of capitalism.

It all began on 29 March, 1957 when Marshal Zhukov visited Berlin. He spoke to political leaders, gave speeches and, while he spoke to political leaders and gave speeches, he did what every Marshal Zhukov did when visiting Berlin: he strutted his stuff for the benefit of American spies. I sometimes think the only point of such speech making in Berlin was to provide material for the double, triple or quadruple agents every country sent to bedevil Germany. A member of the Party even said they shouldn't send so many because there soon wouldn't be any flats left in Berlin for Berliners. It was still a city in ruins and too many people were already complaining of having nowhere to live.

Never mind, back to that file . . . Point 7 of the report recounted how the marshal said the Russian army ought to be prepared to take the initiative if faced by an imminent escalation of tension by the enemy. Nothing new there; the usual song-and-dance. The Pentagon was also telling its spies not to send so many reports, because space was at a premium even in the United States. Moreover, the source was a spy who was useless, like most of the spies reporting from Berlin: to get some payment for their information they would have said they were intending to send a dog into space or any such nonsense they felt was either red hot or freezing cold in Berlin.

If it weren't for a second report that hasn't been declassified, now slumbering in the most secret crannies of the archives of both superpowers, that would have been the end of the matter. Now, of course, everything is up for grabs, is *so* easy, and can be questioned, but at the time the second report was passed up the line until it reached the Oval Office. As Washington and Moscow were at once the mirror and its reflection, the reports written by Russian spies also climbed to the top floor in the Kremlin and crossed the threshold of the President's Office. If the first report, about Zhukov strutting his stuff, was entirely inoffensive, the second was very alarming – it included a map of the United States with all the places marked where the Russians might have stockpiled material for constructing rockets. The map was quite inexact. Moreover, when the U.S. secret services went into action, they only found one hiding-place and that could simply have been bait.

Some people now say it was all the brainwave of a couple of spies who wanted to ensure work didn't run out. A Russian and an American, who had met during the war and reckoned that if they filled a couple of caves in Iowa with scrap metal and sent in a report from Berlin they would be able to mine the vein for a good long time.

Russian spies alerted the Kremlin to the fact that the Americans were desperately seeking the arms caches, a circumstance that enabled the Kremlin to leak maps and more maps of the U.S.A. that were covered in dots. You don't have to remember the Rosenbergs or McCarthy to know how suspicious the guys in Washington can be. You could see at a glance that some were obviously fake, no way could there be armaments inside the Statue of Liberty, in the basement of the White House or under the letters of HOLLYWOOD . . . But some were for real and from time to time they did find a pit, a well or a hole that could be used to hide arms or build a rocket pad. The spies' partners dug holes and purchased scrap metal throughout the United States.

To cut to the chase, drums rolled for summit meetings rather than for war. Secret delegations were sent to Geneva. Geneva, Switzerland . . . At the opposite ends of Europe, dictatorships in countries suppurating in pus. Portugal, Spain, the U.S.S.R. . . . . And in the middle, that great paradise of order, peace and cleanliness (provided you don't peek into their banks, that is) . . . Geneva. Secret talks, as I was saying . . .

Well, to call them secret is an exaggeration verging on deceit, but something of that nature did take place. In these gatherings, the Russian negotiator tried to play Mr Nice, spoke of the possibility that some of his men had acted in the United States without the green light from Moscow, etcetera.

"You know what young men are like, they all want promotion and you can be never sure what they will get up to."

And his counterpart told him he was sceptical about the authenticity of the finds.

"It's not that we don't accept them, but anything of that kind would be a reason to go to war, and it isn't as if we have found anything to worry about in Dakota, but, even so . . ."

"Well, if there is nothing to worry about, no need to waste our time."

"No, of course, on the other hand, all these maps that have come our way do reveal that an interest does exist on your part . . ."

"I don't know what you are talking about. Maps? What maps?"

And the meeting went on, and on, and on, and the hands on patient Swiss clocks moved slowly and Swiss tranquillity in Geneva became ever more tranquil. Two, three, four hours went by and the negotiators were back where they started.

"I haven't a clue which maps you are talking about," reiterated the Russian negotiator.

"No, obviously, as these maps our guys sent us are quite unimportant."

"Road maps? Tourist maps? Weather forecasts?"

"Don't act dumb, the maps of the whereabouts of arms caches."

"If it's arms, we deny everything, naturally . . ."

And hours and more hours went by, six, seven, eight . . . They started to talk about the weather in Switzerland and then returned to the maps.

"If you go public, we will deny everything."

"We won't go public, it was impossible there could be anything. We simply wanted to be reassured you weren't intending to ..."

"'Impossible' is a word that inside the K.G.B. can lead to Siberia, my dear sir ..."

"But, of course, it is impossible for anyone to bring missiles into the United States."

And the hours on the Swiss clocks got longer and longer, and the conversation went round and round like the hands on the Swiss clocks ...

"Nothing is ever impossible, my dear sir ..."

"Oh yes it is ..."

"No, nothing ever is. It could well be that some of our men decided to take it into their own hands to ..." And now the Russian *was* stoking the fire.

And, at that juncture, the American negotiator, quite unawares, said something he should never have said: "Look, General Secretary, you having arms caches in Michigan or Oregon is as impossible as Elvis Presley giving a concert in Red Square."

And the Russian negotiator responded in a way he should never have responded. How could it occur to him? How could he wag his tongue and utter these words?: "In this respect, Red Square in Moscow will always be at the disposition of Elvis Presley, providing he accepts our invitation, naturally. In respect of the arms caches, the logic of the declarations ..."

The two negotiators began to sweat and shake at the mere thought of the expressions on the faces of the members of both delegations who were surely following the conversation via the thousands of microphones that survive the thousand daily searches, heaven knows how.

"So be it," said the American, realising he couldn't withdraw his proposal.

97

"So be it," replied his opposite number.

They say that when the two men said goodbye they were convinced they would never meet again. Their careers in shreds, one saw himself in a traffic department in the Nebraska outback and the other at a low-level desk in Sakhalin.

Elvis Presley in Red Square . . . The scourge of American morality meets the enemy of the United States after the Second World War: together in a single performance. The Russian authorities couldn't let slip an opportunity like that. Contrary to what he was expecting, their negotiator was given a promotion on his return to Moscow. He couldn't believe it, but the truth was it was the fruit of a strategy concocted while he was flying back from Geneva. If they sent him to Siberia, the Americans would find out sooner or later and then they would think it was all the fault of that garrulous guy, "What kind of staff do those Russians employ? Do they marinate their brains in vodka or what?" they imagined them saying. On the contrary, if they promoted him, it would mean his challenge had the backing of the whole Party – forgive the redundant adjective, dear reader: the Party, in Russia, is always the "whole" Party – and were hanging on a response from Washington.

In the United States President Eisenhower gathered together the best and most discreet brains from around the country. It wasn't only a concert that was at stake: the statement made by the negotiator, listened to a million times by the intelligence services, was entirely credible and they continued filtering maps as if they were dropping from the guttering of the worst *izba* in the entire Russian steppes. They finally managed to demonstrate it was all a fabrication – though they continued to discover suspicious objects that sustained the search for several months more – but it was too late to back out of the game. In the words of Ike himself: "No Russian ain't going to show us how to play poker."

It was a serious wager, and for a time people even thought it must be a way of defusing the tension around issues that really preoccupied both governments, a manoeuvre by moderate sectors in both countries. It wasn't. It was a genuine bet that had both secret services clocking up overtime. The best of it was that the majority of spies were working in the dark; nobody imagined that a rock concert could be driving that peculiar operation. Why do they want the list of the top hits in Albuquerque, wondered some puzzled spies. And that wasn't all: in the K.G.B. everyone was beginning to decipher secret message after secret message in the lyrics, in music reviews in the newspapers, in the magazines for the sector . . . In other words: a stack of work.

Elvis in Red Square . . . The scourge of American morality at the heart of the empire of evil . . . before his spell in the army, naturally.

On 10 December, 1957 Elvis Presley received a letter from the armed forces. The navy was offering to create a unit named "Elvis Presley" if he enlisted as a volunteer before his draft time came. Elvis delayed his entry into the ranks. He was not informed of the motive and, naturally, the murky figure of Colonel Parker was always by his side. Ah, Colonel Parker . . . There was some talk of possibly eliminating him, but it was the usual tune, Russian espionage would use such a step as evidence that things weren't quite right in Washington. In the end, the general staff decided Elvis should be sent to Germany, a sacrifice of two years, to prepare the concert in Red Square. He – and the Colonel even more so – feared it would be the end of his career, but they received guarantees that when he returned to America he would be welcomed as the greatest singer of all time.

While the Americans were preparing their ground, two versions did the rounds in Russia, both endorsed by metre after metre of reports. Some said the Americans would call it off. No way. As it wouldn't become public, they preferred to let it roll – no-one would ever find out and if word did come out, it wouldn't have an ounce of credibility:

who would be so crazy as to think Elvis had performed in Red Square?

The others, on the other hand, were confident the Americans had picked up the gauntlet. Korea was Korea and Elvis was Elvis. They weren't in any mood to lose the war of dispatches, if they were taking their time, it was because they wanted to win the contest and hear "Blue Suede Shoes" being sung against the same backdrop as those interminable military parades. Neither negotiator had agreed a date or a programme; consequently both were still there for the taking.

The second version gradually gained credibility. Elvis not only joined the army, he was assigned to a military base in Germany in September 1958. The Russians couldn't believe it. What's more, the Americans sent press and television too. The Devil's best strategy is to act as if he doesn't exist. That's my cliché, by the way, though I am sure the K.G.B. must have used it in some report or other.

In Moscow, we – and I say "we" because I was there by now – weren't exactly calm either. The problem was that they were only staking a man, we were staking a country: it wasn't an even match. We were thinking – well, I was there but I wasn't thinking – that we were playing on home ground; though the Americans' nerve at sending Elvis to Germany was causing our bosses headaches. There was enough paper in the reports written on the movements of possible Elvises – maybe he had a double, maybe he didn't – to wallpaper all the flats under construction in Berlin.

Our bosses analysed all the possibilities. Initially they considered offering the Americans the option of a concert inside the Kremlin. The Americans would win a point, they could say they had managed to bring it off inside the Kremlin, in the presence of Khrushchev himself, but the idea was thrown out a couple of weeks later; it was too obvious the Americans might think a concert inside the walls of the Kremlin wasn't much of a coup: the wager stipulated Red Square. The Americans had insisted the concert should take place without fail in Red Square with the same loudspeakers Elvis usually used, the same outfits he usually wore, all exactly the same as in the U.S. of A. . . . . What hadn't been discussed was the audience. In the U.S. of A., there was usually an audience, but that issue hadn't been raised . . .

Our bosses had a response ready. If the Americans wanted an audience, they could have one. Elvis would be faced by the massed ranks of the orchestras of Moscow, Kiev and St Petersburg playing a selection of numbers by Tchaikovsky. That could be fun, could even be broadcast. What a humiliation for the capitalist star system for its singer to have to bawl behind the combined orchestras of Moscow, St Petersburg and Kiev! They would bring in all the choirs in the U.S.S.R. to drown out the American rock star's loudspeakers.

While the details of the concert were being ironed out, a thousand encounters were held. The world was in a bad state. Recent events in Taiwan, the conflicts in the East and the situation in Cuba absorbed the negotiating energies of both superpowers, but neither dropped the wager. That challenge was a kind of subterranean river that flowed beneath every meeting convened. The visits of ambassadors to Moscow, and even Nixon's visit, contained reference to the wager. Moreover, the first negotiators in the matter held important positions in their respective governments and conducted business simultaneously as a personal and national issue. Taiwan was the item on the agenda but in the end, as if it were the result of a game haunting both sides, mention was always made of Elvis in Red Square.

Consequently, they had to play it calmly, and, on instructions from Eisenhower and Khrushchev, the subject became a question of national priority. Sputnik had damaged the morale of the United States, so every opportunity to deliver a counterpunch had to be grasped. E.S. – the Elvis Section – was set up in the Pentagon, copying what the navy had

unsuccessfully tried to do months before. They created an Elvis squad –
carried out pioneering aesthetic surgery and gave singing and combat
training. A throng of cowboy-shirted soldiers with greasy toupees
practising the martial arts – what a sight! You wouldn't credit the
things we have seen. The K.G.B. was sent a bunch of photos.

In the meantime, Elvis's every move in Germany was scrutinised by
an irritated yet intrigued media. In the end, the show dragged. Colonel
Parker was put on a short (very short) tether, no-one could allow the
greed of this individual to ruin that intricate ballet of moves and
countermoves.

And they weren't exactly quiet in Moscow either. Scientists were
working night and day to create paint able to absorb sound, a varnish
that could be applied to the paving in the square, to the walls of the
Kremlin and even to the domes of St. Basil's Cathedral. The noise from
the concert was a real headache, and multiple – and, it has to be said,
highly curious – solutions were dreamt up to deal with that gig: a
couple of university chairs were created to study the question of sound
absorption.

The Red Army even started to shift soldiers for some apparently
crucial manoeuvres in Moscow. In Moscow! Manoeuvres! And not just
anywhere in Moscow: right on the Kremlin's doorstep. There were
foreign agents who speculated about the possibility of a coup, but
when they started to look for heirs and new members of the Politburo,
it didn't add up. They drew the strangest assumptions. And, naturally,
wrote a bunch of reports.

The K.G.B. also created an "Elvis Presley" section with agents who
dyed their hair so it wasn't so fair. Suffice it to say that their attempts
at realistic imitation – efforts that in the Pentagon's case were highly
successful – were less than adequate. Never in the history of the Soviet
Union had so much American music been listened to as in those

K.G.B. offices. Lyrics were dissected left, right and centre; genealogies, stanza formation and melodies were subject to critical analysis. Leading composers were invited in to explain the success of the lyrics. It didn't last long. Obviously, as soon as the composers entered K.G.B. head-quarters, they only praised the Russian tradition and poured scorn on capitalist music that could bring no good; all their explanations were in similar vein. It was little help.

In the meantime, the day that had been set for the spectacle was approaching. It had been extremely difficult to find a date to suit every-body. Needless to say, Elvis was not consulted; he would go whenever, and that was that. The fact is that, according to the reports coming through, the boy was rather dejected; "soft in the head" would be more accurate. His mother had died not that long ago, he had finally found the woman who would be his wife, Priscilla, and he wasn't at his best. At that time, two hundred C.I.A. agents were accompanying Elvis around Germany. No less than sixty men slept next door to his private house near the base. His companions in the division were replaced by boys considered to be clean: youths unpolluted by anything Russian, be it surnames, family holidays or hobbies. By anything at all.

As I was saying, the agreed day was approaching: a Tuesday in November 1958. There couldn't be enough preparations, given that neither side seemed ready to yield an inch. One lot continued to defy them and wanted Elvis merely to travel to Moscow and the others stood their ground and demanded a rock concert in Red Square.

They agreed a pact of non-aggression. The plane would meet no obstacles in landing and taking off. MiGs would escort it as soon as it flew over the Iron Curtain and the same MiGs would escort it back. They didn't want anything to go wrong. The Russian leaders even thought there might be an American strategy to crash the plane in Russian territory: they could see the headlines already: "Kidnapped

Elvis dies in Russian air crash". No, they could take no chances. Only the best pilots and the best flying machines.

The K.G.B. commissioned a huge tarpaulin for Lenin's mausoleum. A cover made of the highest-grade echo-resistant material, so nothing would be heard inside. The loudspeakers the technicians tested a month before the big day were the same make as those Elvis used in his recent concerts in the U.S.A. Once the embalmed Lenin was safely sheathed – leading members of the Politburo vigorously debated the sacrilege of disturbing Lenin's eternal sleep – the most pressing concern was that nobody should see Elvis perform. They were less worried that somebody might catch a ripple of sound from the concert. Besides, there was the excuse of the manoeuvres in the Kremlin. The concert, all in all, wouldn't last more than an hour and a half.

So, once Red Square and the Kremlin were evacuated, all they had to do was to let Elvis perform.

And the day came.

Six aeroplanes left one of the bases the Americans still have in Germany, two flew to Helsinki, two to Athens and two to Moscow. Putting the enemy off the scent . . . Of course, nobody was: that was their normal procedure. In their final negotiations they had agreed that two planes would land in the airport.

They transported Elvis from the airport to Red Square in a helicopter that landed by the side of Saint Basil's Cathedral. It had long been cleared of locals and tourists by the time he arrived. The K.G.B. had designed a perfectly orchestrated formation so that the diverse ranks of agents – from general to private – exited in such a way that not one of them actually saw Elvis. In the report it says only one person managed to see his face. Nobody knows who he was and nobody wrote his name down anywhere . . . It could be anybody . . . It could be me . . .

It *was* me.

I was mandated to keep an eye on the electrical equipment in case a connection failed. The slightest interruption of the concert would be considered an act of sabotage. Elvis started testing. And those words "One, two, three", "One, two, three" rang out, and then one more time, until he started singing "Heartbreak Hotel".

He followed up with "Hound Dog". The truth is it was quite something seeing him up on stage in the empty square. It was cold, naturally, but I could see he was sweating. He danced while I hummed the songs silently to myself. I must have been less than twenty metres from the front of the stage, but my back was turned. I was only allowed to take an occasional glance to check that it was working, that the spotlights were still on, and that no electric cable had worked loose. The music sounded very loud from where I was, but one could intuit that two hundred yards further away, the reverberation from the walls and façades rendered unintelligible all the words I had learned as a result of hearing them so often, day after day, week after week, for going on a year.

Whenever I turned round, I could see him sweating, could see him swaying as we had seen him sway in the films we had been made to see in the section. But it was really quite pathetic. A guy, all alone, half disguised as a cowboy in the middle of the stage, playing his guitar and singing. In an empty square. Well, with only me there, with my back to him, turning round now and then to ensure everything was working. The black sheath on Lenin's mausoleum. The aeroplanes flying over Moscow.

When it finished, I disconnected the current as per orders and the helicopter appeared in a flash, took off again and transported him to the aeroplane that was to fly him back to Germany.

Nothing more was heard of the affair. Nobody ever mentioned it again, because people were scared – and not a little shamefaced.

THE RUSSIAN ENCYCLOPAEDIA

This is the story of events that took place in the capital of our vast empire.

The daily routine on the fourth floor of the National Publishing Archive went like this: as soon as the editorial assistants finished checking the entries, they handed every document over to the fact checkers who, when they had signed their approval, sent them on to the spelling checkers. The copy editors handed them to the political commissars and, after they had given their political verdict, they were in turn obliged to send the final versions to higher bodies, the apparatchiks of which assigned a mark to each entry. Zero was for those that weren't at all dangerous: flowers, dogs, or oesophagus. One was for those that might have some kind of ideological implications: energy, architecture or philosophy. Two was more complicated and was only used to place entries nobody knew where to place. A three was given to specific biographies of famous individuals and four was awarded only to concepts that had to be revisited every two years: revolution, state, nation, party, religion, people, and so on.

The documents were lodged in different filing cabinets in alphabetical order, and porters immediately sealed the drawers and took them up to the top floor, except for those marked with a four, which went straight to the sixth floor. The others were processed, photocopied, certified and, finally, set and dispatched to the printer as an exact, countersigned copy. Every one of the sheets that the editors had written, all the entries and corrections, were filed on the first and second floors where more and more corridors full of filing cabinets led to huge rooms full of filing cabinets. The signs hanging from the ceiling gave precise directions so no-one could get lost – headings and nomenclatures that were there to guide the civil servants working in the archival area as well as the different porters who ran up and down the whole building searching for a specific entry or photograph.

Because there wasn't merely a section for entries and definitions; there was also a section for photographs, and one for drawings, and another for charts and maps, and all these sections housed the biennial revisions. And even more important than any of those was the section for referrals to other archives held at the Higher Council for Science and Technology, at the Centre for Research into Historical Materialism, at the National Organ for the Arts and Literature, and at an infinite number of institutions, departments and ministries, agencies and offices, all recorded in the special filing cabinets on the first floor.

The Foreign Affairs archive was on the third floor. It was the least consulted. One needed a special pass that was only issued by the editors who dealt with that area. All the information from abroad that was necessary in order to write entries for the national encyclopaedias was there, and that information alone.

Order and discipline were everywhere. The strict procedures ruling the archives seemed to have entered the blood of every single civil servant, official, recorder, secretary and assessor. Total silence reigned; the distance between workers made it impossible to hold a conversation, people would have been forced to bawl from one end to the other, and everyone would have frowned upon that.

Ossip Yakovlevitch worked on the fourth floor in the editorial section of the National Encyclopaedia. His was a peaceful section: body sciences, nothing special. He was responsible for writing up the entries for definitions in the ear, throat and, above all, nose department. The

Otorhinolaryngological Medicine Department communicated to his section the reports and directives it considered opportune. He ordered the reports, made detailed precis and then immediately sent them for filing. When he had to revise the entries, he added in the most important changes and scientific innovations. And what changes those simple words suffered . . . Ah, "sinusitis"! Every year he received thousands of articles written by the best doctors in the Union . . . And "disphony", what a wonderful article on the impact of air on the vocal chords, ah . . .

Ossip knew everything about the larynx. He knew everything you could know about the eardrum and its afflictions – size, weight, parts, tissue, just as he knew about the pituitary gland and the vocal chords. He knew the names, lives and miracles of the scientists who had described how those organs worked. He remembered the figures and carried in his head many of the photographs surgeons used to explain their operations. By way of example, when he thought of the nose, his head would be awash with such disparate details as eighteenth-century engravings describing every possible type of nose or some of the diseases that deprived men of their noses. He had seen every kind, had read about every colour and could have been a Professor of Noses or Ears in any university in the country.

Ossip Yakovlevitch only ever interacted with Vitali Prokov, who had been his messenger for the last year, an excellent worker who went up and down the many stairs with total diligence. They had transferred him to the fourth floor, and Ossip didn't know why, but he was always hovering around his table. He was a competent fellow who delivered and filed reports in next to no time, faultless in his knowledge of corridors and filing cabinet areas, of desks and trays and the face of almost every civil servant on every floor. He had never let him down, always found the required document, always got the permission signed and always returned to the job with exemplary speed. Ossip was delighted he had got Vitali and not that tramp Konstantin. Vitali was friendly, never rude, was in fact extremely pleasant. It was impossible to get any work done with a porter who was dim: you could waste hours.

Absolutely . . . Once he had had to help the civil servant responsible for the respiratory system because his porter had such a backlog of work he couldn't keep abreast of it. Ossip and Vitali had to do the others' work. Ossip defined the alveolus and trachea and Vitali had to stand in for Konstantin, who had more alcohol than blood flowing in his veins. Everybody thought he would die from internal combustion and suspected him of having several bottles of vodka stashed at the back of some filing cabinets, but no-one had ever found them. Konstantin possibly knew the building better than anyone. Konstantin was the exception, however, though he usually bumbled through his assignments.

In fact, everything had to be right because there was a rule that said it had to be right, or else . . . All the documents had to be signed by those who had been involved, and that is how they knew there was strict control, that any error, any incomplete or wrongly corrected file, any evidence of incompetence, could be used against one by one's superiors and – it wouldn't be the first time – also by a lower-level civil servant who wanted to prosper on the backs of those above them.

It was a restlessly restful life, Ossip Yakovlevitch liked to tell his friends when they came to dinner, "An erroneous definition of the neck and they'll cut yours off, they'll drop you down a grade," was one of his favourite, oft-repeated quips to describe his situation at the National Archive. According to one of his bosses, they were "the guarantors of the nation's knowledge, because the state printed what they revised, changed and wrote every year and distributed it to the four corners of the Union". Ossip Yakovlevitch would stand on his chair, point a finger at the ceiling, at the light, and imitate his director: "The definition of the nose is the bedrock of the Union." He would end his imitations with "Oh, keep your nose to the grindstone and get on with life, like everyone else". The life of Ossip Yakovlevitch held no secrets or mysteries: his was banal happiness, the restlessly restful life that was the story of Russia itself.

Until the day came that changed everything.

Vitali Prokov left a note on his table. He had been summoned to the seventh floor – the seventh floor! – that same morning at twelve o'clock. The seventh floor, the seventh floor, the seventh floor . . . And that was the last he saw of Vitali Prokov that morning. He stood up from time to time and looked over the filing cabinets, but he was nowhere to be seen. The seventh floor. Whenever he read the note, he went into a cold sweat. Besides, it was half past nine . . .

He got nothing done the whole morning. He kept looking at the summons, seventh floor, Ossip Yakovlevitch, at twelve on the dot, office number six . . . The note began to wrinkle he touched it so often, unfolding and folding it back into its envelope. Restlessly restless. Luckily the filing cabinets hid him from sight and no-one could see him, flushed, in a sweat, nervous and anxious from so much rereading of that seventh-floor summons. . . Nonetheless, when he got up to go to the lavatory, he thought the other civil servants were looking at him. Perhaps they know, he thought. He couldn't even tell his wife he was wanted on the seventh floor, at twelve.

At last it struck a quarter to.

Ossip took the lift. He wasn't allowed to, but thought that if he was going up to the seventh floor he might as well. And he did, and pressed number seven, much to the surprise and confusion of the editors for bones and muscles, the ones sitting closest to the lift. As he went up, he wondered why he had done so, given that he wasn't allowed to, but he was so nervous he had pressed the buttons for every floor so the lift stopped at every level.

There was an expanse of thick, brown carpet on the seventh floor, ultra-soft and clean as if it were brand new. It was the first time he had been up there. He had always wondered what they must do on this rarefied level. He sat on one of the sofas in the corridor and waited. He felt calmer now, but while he waited he mentally reviewed all the recent entries he had written and projects he had been assigned. He could find nothing out of the ordinary. He could not recall a single error that merited a summons to the seventh. Not one. Perhaps he had made a few edits in the entry on the trachea written by another civil servant responsible for the respiratory system, but that was it, and that was hardly enough to take him to the seventh.

All the same, there he was at the top, in the corridor, sitting on one of the sofas, when a door suddenly opened and a young lady emerged and called out his name.

"Ossip Yakovlevitch, please do come in!" Ossip got up, walked into the room the young lady had emerged from and when he went to give her the summons, she shook her head and told him to wait inside.

No-one was in the room. There was a long table with a decorative samovar in the centre and lots of empty chairs. He was there a good ten minutes waiting for someone to appear, standing up, not daring to sit down on any of the chairs. In fact, he didn't dare budge from the spot. He glanced back at the summons, the seventh floor, Ossip Yakovlevitch, twelve o'clock, and put it away again.

Then he heard chairs being moved in the adjacent room, and soon afterwards, voices. The door opened and three men walked in, one being Vitali Prokov. Ah, thought Ossip. What can *he* have told them? Nothing, because I've not done anything wrong . . .

"Do be seated, Ossip Ossipovitch Yakovlevitch, please do be seated," said the man who looked the most important member of the trio.

All three sat at the other end of the table, and the man in the middle continued speaking, even though Ossip couldn't see him because he was hidden behind the samovar. So, the samovar went on to describe Ossip's achievements, C.V., career and services rendered, even details that weren't really relevant, like his wife's job and the school their children attended, the date when he ordered the car that was yet to be delivered, etc.

"Ossip Ossipovitch Yakovlevitch, you must be wondering why we have summoned you," said the samovar.

"Sir, I . . . well, of course, sir, I received the summons and . . ."

"We want you to come and work on the sixth floor, Yakovlevitch, we want you to collaborate with us in writing and redefining category four concepts. Mr Anatoli Ditriavin –" an arm extended from behind the samovar and pointed at Vitali Prokov, who chuckled – "has given us many good reports about your work. You have scrupulously attended to every single project assigned to you over the last twelve years. He even told us how you reacted when the porter Konstantin delayed the work of your colleague. We are very happy with your work and we think you can continue in the same vein on the sixth. You will answer to the senior editorial committee. You know that teachers and professors come from all over the country to define the central thrust of our publications and we need competent and, above all, discreet staff."

Ossip kept nodding, it was all he could do while the other went on. Finally, the man moved his chair slightly to one side and looked him in the face.

"The samovar is bolted to the table, we can't move it, don't worry." He was now looking into his face. "We are very happy with your work, but now you will have to prove that you can take on greater challenges than defining a nose. We hope you can rise to the necessary level. Anatoli will bring you your new contract and go through the detail of the change. Do you have any questions? Any doubts? No, that's excellent, then. Take the rest of the day off and come up to the sixth floor tomorrow."

And they left the same way they had entered. Anatoli grinned at him.

So, he could be pleased with himself. That meant he was going up in rank, that he would earn more, that they could ask to change flats and bring forward delivery of the car. He went down in the lift and, before going down, pressed the buttons to every floor. He tidied the papers on his desk and went off home, grinning like a cat that had found the cream.

Next morning he shaved with the utmost care, put on his best clothes and arrived at work five minutes before he used to when he went to the fourth floor. Aha, twelve years describing ears and noses, and now here I am on my way up to the sixth. No more noses and ears, from now on: the Union, the Republic, and most likely even Socialism or Revolution . . . And all those political science professors. No more editing articles and studies written by common-or-garden surgeons. He was fed up with dealing with petty academics who wanted their names in the National Encyclopaedia because they had discovered the bacteria that inflamed the veins inside tonsils. Tonsils, I ask you! Who is interested in tonsils!

Anatoli congratulated him, but Ossip didn't dare to ask him more than was strictly necessary. Anatoli was no longer a porter. He held some much higher rank and Ossip wanted no dealings with his superiors – he never had had and didn't want to start now. The work was very similar to what he did before and he would soon adapt.

The sixth floor was similar to the fourth, except that the filing cabinets reached the ceiling. They didn't simply receive articles from within the nation, as on the fourth, but were often sent books and articles from abroad. As he knew French, they delivered to him documents written in that language, and he immediately wrote a precis, noting if they referred to communism, socialism, anarchism, Marxism, Leninism, Maoism, or if they talked about freedom, libertarianism, liberation etc., etc., etc. He had stopped picking noses, he would tell his wife when he came home, and stopped cleaning out earholes – and he would laugh; now he dealt with the most important words in history.

Even though Ossip began dynamically, in great spirit, after the first round of novelties, days went by and were completely lacklustre; his table, his chair, the photocopies of forms, the chrome table lamp where he could see reflections of the filing cabinets, the table, the photocopied forms and himself, his forehead and nose being the centre of that shiny, convex surface. Every day, Ossip switched on his table lamp, tidied the entries and the precis of the definitions and immediately rang his bell in order to summon Vassili, with whom he had the most courteous of relationships, just in case he was a civil servant from the seventh keeping an eye on him, heaven forbid. He preferred not to think about it, and that was why he always had everything ready to rule out the possibility of mistakes. So, time went by, just the same as on the third. The only difference was the quantity and density of the articles that came his way, that Vassili then filed away; planning, planners, development plans, five-year development plans and more of the same, endlessly.

Until the day finally dawned when they convened the biennial review and Ossip donned his best clothes and waited with the other civil servants on the sixth floor for the committee of wise men to arrive. Each of them had to bring along the annual résumé of the new developments around the six concepts. It worked the same as on the fourth floor;

everyone had their specific remit for their endeavours. They all had to bring along the articles describing new developments, the summaries of two years of editing and working in their respective fields. Vassili accompanied him. The porters stood behind their chairs in case they had to fetch a document. Each civil servant had a table assigned where the reports on the concepts that were their responsibility had been set out. Right from the start Ossip had been given the entries on economy, work, development, inflation, depression and balance of trade. He laid out small piles of articles and reports opposite each chair, and waited for them to arrive.

The professors who came and talked to him congratulated him for his diligence, order and neatness, asked him what floor he had previously worked on and were very pleasant. They weren't much interested in him. In fact, they spoke much more to each other; they rarely met, and took advantage of these encyclopaedia days to catch up.

"Well, you must have seen how economic terms are very different from . . . Now, what was it that you said you used to do?"

"Otorhinolaryngology, sir, the ear, nose and throat department."

"Oh, right, ear, nose and throat, yes, you've seen how there's much more work to do here."

"Yes, sir, I have."

"And how all this is much more important."

"Very much more so, sir, indeed, very much more so."

"You must reflect, dear Yakov Ossipovitch, that what we do here is to define the importance of the words that rule our lives. Hey, but don't be offended, we're not tweaking your ear," quipped another professor.

"No, sir, I have seen how different the work is, how hugely important it is, and I hope, modestly, sir, to see to the duties my superiors have seen fit to entrust me with, sir. I am proud to be able to serve you and contribute with my efforts to the development of the National Encyclopaedia, sir."

"Excellent, Ossipovitch, excellent."

And then the professors started talking among themselves about everything they had been doing over the last two years, excellent, Ossipovitch, excellent. And went on discussing the importance of their activities and research and the research centres they were directing and their universities and the bonuses that work brought them. After ordering the porter to bring coffee and chatting a little more, they took away the documents they each thought relevant.

"Goodbye, Mr Ossipovitch, we will let you know the changes that should be made. Enjoy yourself and see you in a couple of years."

"Goodbye, gentlemen, I look forward to receiving your comments. I will read them with the utmost pleasure."

And that was that.

In the days subsequent to the meeting, articles and, in particular, more texts kept coming to the tables that dealt with the agricultural sector, demographic changes to avoid unemployment, various professorial statistical accounts and studies of the dynamic levers of the economy. Until the day came when the envelopes began to arrive with the modifications for each of the terms, all with the identical comment: "The definitions in the National Encyclopaedia should be maintained, new developments in the current biennial period are not sufficiently important to warrant changing any of the terms in which the definitions are expressed." Indeed, there was no need to alter anything. They were the same definitions that had been established in the very first round. In forty years, nobody had dared to change a single word of the definitions. Naturally, the paperwork kept piling up in the filing cabinets that Vassili organised so conscientiously, and he kept stamping and signing the documents that registered their validity, he who had read them from cover to cover, who knew the economies of every territory in the Soviet Union like the back of his hand and who was responsible, he saw clearly enough, for preserving unchanged the definitions that been thought valid from the very start, year after year, decade after decade.

Oh, and the nose . . .

THE LONELIEST MAN IN THE WORLD

After circling the world for three days, after travelling further from humanity than any cosmonaut before him, he woke up and saw that the world was still down there, quiet, like the back of a huge slumbering monster.

Lev Riazanov was intelligent enough to understand that he had gone into orbit after he had spun round and round for three days without anyone being able to change the direction of his spaceship. Base headquarters insisted they were doing everything possible to discover the source of the breakdown and what they might do to modify the course of the ship. They could say what they liked down there, but *he* couldn't figure out any solution.

He had switched off the transmitter and slept continuously for eight hours. He had removed all the sensors from his chest and wrists as well as from his temples. He had been longing to sleep without cables trailing all over his body and waking him up every five minutes. For two days! The moment he went into orbit and one of his engines crashed, when he realised the situation was grim and that if he didn't go out and repair it with his own two hands, he was stuck in one hell of a fix. He didn't want to listen to anyone, the idiots at the base were the last straw, he was sick of hearing them sing that same old song, the protocol to follow in situations like that. He knew it by heart, who did they think they were talking to? To some civilian pilot? He had six space flights and six landings behind him! Did they reckon he was a child who needed all the manual instructions rehearsed time and again when he knew them by heart? He was sick of base, disconnected the radio and went to sleep in the gravity-free cabin.

Like a child. He loved gravity-free sleep. It was like falling asleep in the heated swimming pool when they were doing exercises to prepare for being gravity-free. He had fallen asleep more than once. It was also true enough that there was always some bastard who cut off his air supply and he had had to jettison his mask and swim to the surface . . . He had fallen asleep like a child. What with the stress, exhaustion and the fools at the base. They had been riling him for two nights, he should look at this, look at that, our best scientists are reviewing the situation, keep calm because we're on the case. "The causes and effects of the breakdown your bloody mother experienced when she brought you into the world, you shit-face," Captain Riazanov told the people at the base, not giving what he said a second thought.

They had been on his back for two days. He had checked all the controls, the circuits, the leads, the tubes, the connections, the switches and the keyboards and cables that surrounded him on every side, shiny surfaces where little lights flickered just as they did outside through the window. In fact, what a load of scrap that can was, he had seen tanks better equipped. And certainly more comfortable. He had cut himself at least five times on sharp edges the lazy lot at base hadn't smoothed off. Sure, he could keep reviewing . . . "Now look at the levels of . . . Now check that the indicators aren't . . . Be patient, we think we've got it, it may be . . . Please, Captain Riazanov, don't insult us, behave properly, it doesn't become a person such as yourself."

"Well, we'll soon find out about that, Commander Get-it-up-the-arse, I'm going to sleep right now," had been his last response to the chiefs at base who couldn't believe their ears; he was so exhausted and tired of fiddling with the entrails of his spaceship. He disconnected the radio – an act punishable by six months behind bars and disqualification from any kind of mission, according to protocol number . . . and went off to sleep.

As soon as he woke up, he ate some of that freeze-dried rubbish, a couple of ration packs, double the amount recommended by those idiots who had never travelled up here and didn't know how stressed and frightened you got and how hungry that made you. He sat back in his seat and looked through the glass panels. Oh, how wonderful it was up here, there was nothing comparable, all those years of work and study, all those years of self-discipline and competing with other cosmonauts, finally bore fruit, a round fruit, perfectly round and multi-coloured. And the moon, and the sun. He simply sat down to check that nothing had changed, the earth was still spinning round like a top, the moon and the sun appeared and disappeared, just like the earth, but more quickly. Now we're a foursome, he thought. You three and me.

Captain Lev Riazanov gathered his last resources of patience and pressed the radio button. It had been disconnected all night, but what a drag, what a drag to be forced to listen to that collection of incompetent fools. Please, if you can't find solutions, at least you could have learned how to check the spaceship. Civil servants! he was thinking as he hesitated over whether to press the button until in the end. Bah! Click.

"Captain Lev Riazanov, Captain Lev Riazanov, can you hear us? Are you well? We find your behaviour extremely distressing. Don't disconnect the radio again, you know that according to the protocol . . ."

"Yes, of course I do, you fool, I just wondered if you had found out what the problem is and know how to put it right. I'll make it easier for you and make my request in two parts. One: have you got anywhere? Two: idiot!"

"Captain Riazanov, I beg you not to insult me. We are doing every-thing we can to discover the source of the mechanical dysfunction that caused . . ."

Click.

Yes. The engines had crashed, the first had led to the meltdown of the second and there was no way his ship could leave the orbit it had now entered. In other words, he was circling like an unmanned satel-lite. He could go round and round the earth indefinitely, for ever and ever. The problem was as old as Newton himself: the force with which two bodies are attracted to each other and all that ensues, the theory demonstrating that, if one travels at a certain height above the earth at a certain speed, then one continues in like mode indefinitely, the ABC of the theory of gravity. The body in question (the spaceship) would carry on, and wouldn't leave its orbit until the imperfections of physics sent it off course. And then the situation would hardly improve; there were only two options: it would either fall to earth or else it would whiz into outer space.

It was that simple and clear. He had heard Armeniaran, his favourite teacher at the Academy, say as much on a number of occasions. The hapless Armeniaran who "finally had to give up teaching because of persistent nephritic diarrhoea", just one more way of saying he had been purged. Armeniaran would explain equally forcefully the para-bolas and trajectories of the vessels they sent into space and the infighting in the School of Cosmonauts section of the Party.

"If initially you don't know where you are going, or do something you shouldn't, you could be sent into orbit, like a satellite, up on high where no-one will bother you. And if you then decide you want to come out of orbit, you must choose between a) going off into space and freezing or b) launching back and burning up. Your mistakes will find you out, physics is physics," he would say from time to time, when an experiment failed, when the solution to a problem proved incorrect.

"Outer space", as everybody knew, was Siberia. "Launching back" meant that the secret services would give you a party, like a satellite coming back into the atmosphere at a higher speed than expected and burning out.

And Lev Riazanov, one of Armeniaran's favourite pupils, was stuck in orbit. He had so admired Armeniaran, a polite, precise man, "to twenty decimal points, at least, when the decimals aren't recurring". He didn't explain mathematical or physics models, he was a mathematical and physics model. He was theory, pure theory and precise solution, method taken into the nooks and crannies that everyone else forgot. They had burned Armeniaran up, and he was in orbit, the system had to function correctly. Physics is physics.

He remembered learning about most of the failed attempts when he had studied in Moscow. They sent rabbits up in the first satellites. Some came back roasted. There was less said about the manned flights, but evidently everyone talked about them. There were two ways you could fail. The first was down below, namely, the thing exploded at lift-off. The second, on the return journey, the thing exploded when you thought you were home and dry. The students who aspired to be cosmonauts were always debating which was the best option. There were pros and cons on both sides.

He also knew the story of Jossef Uliavnoski, who spun out of orbit and must now be hurtling between the orbits of the planets. The gossips reckoned that the mistake hid a desire for his to be the first spaceship to keep to a planned trajectory over such a long period. That is, Uliavnoski's death was entirely pre-planned. People speculated about the weight of his spaceship, the amount of food he was carrying and much more besides – perhaps they had overstocked his supplies. It was also true Uliavnoski had only ever driven tractors or steered bicycles. But Uliavnoski will never be able to tell us, may his soul rest in peace and his body continue its journey for ever and ever. Lots of jokes were cracked about Uliavnoski! They say the Americans want to send out a probe to gather all kinds of information on the situation in our solar system – just imagine if they find Uliavnoski before the probe . . .

Better stick on in there, thought Lev as he approached the radio three hours later.

"Captain Lev Riazanov, this is an order, don't disconnect the radio," said the voice of his commander-in-chief. Captain Lev had met him at the Academy. Ivan Korobov was the principal. They called him Ivan the Terrible because of his proverbial bad temper and the stress caused by the exams and the tests he set. If heads had to roll, more rolled than necessary. His vigorous voice was spoiling the panorama Lev could see before him: a splendid sunset, the sun was peeping out from behind Africa, and Ivan the Terrible on the phone . . . The Devil exists and has extremely poor taste, thought Captain Riazanov.

"Hey, Ivan, I'm in a jam, got any news? I promise you that if you waste any more of my time fiddling with tubes, I will disconnect the radio until the batteries run out, it's down to you." He heard all the people laugh in the control room when they heard Ivan's response. If their intention was to keep him busy so he didn't think about his situation, they might as well forget it.

"No, Lev, nothing to report as yet. These fools couldn't fly a paper plane, but I promise you we have the best personnel on the case. I have even brought in Shernomirdin, who was in Kola. I'm not trying to trick you, Lev, this is a hard nut to crack."

"So, I will continue freewheeling then."

"Hey, you bastard, don't fuck us around, they're grinding their teeth in Moscow."

"Moscow, O Moscow, how great you think you are and how small you are to me, Moscow, a speck of fly shit . . . No good news, then?"

"I told you, Lev, we are doing what we—"

"I'm going to hang up, Ivan, this is a long-distance call and will cost me the earth. When you've got any news, give me a shout. I'll ring again in four or five hours."

"No, don't."

Click.

That son of a bitch, thought Lev. If he could, he'd have kicked me into outer space, and now he's running scared of the wolves in Moscow. Of course, I'm a hero decorated with all the gongs going in Moscow, stuck in this jalopy thousands of kilometres up and whizzing round faster than a rattle on the day the Dynamos play the final . . . And the people in Moscow must be angry with me for switching off the radio and because by now they must have split their sides laughing in the Pentagon with all the jokes they'll be telling about Captain Lev Riazanov. What's my nickname, I wonder? The bastards must be laughing like . . . And let them get on with it. Their spies must be exhausted after sending in so many reports . . .

And what if I give them a fright and tell them I am one of a range of distractions and that in an hour's time their number will be up, that they have a bunch of mushrooms on the point of eruption? If I mentioned three words, "nuclear bomb imminent", we'd soon see if they'd still be laughing. "Gentlemen of the C.I.A., while you gawp like baboons at me whizzing round and simulating a breakdown, I can inform you that in less than an hour's time the glorious United States will be transformed into the biggest car park in the world," or "Dear President of the United States of America, if you want to see the biggest mushrooms you have ever seen, then just take a look out of the Oval Office." They must be laughing, the captain thought, as if they hadn't fried or lost any cosmonauts, the bastards, come on, Lev, while you're still alive, stir yourself.

Click.

"Attention, please, a message for the head of the U.S. Armed Forces. By this time the missiles that left the Bering Strait must be over Alaska. This satellite was sent into orbit with the express intention of blurring the radar signals. The weather forecast predicts that it will pour down and get hot, very hot. Don't worry, you will end up rich, capitalist gentlemen, your country will be full of opencast uranium and plutonium mines."

Click.

They must be running wild like headless chickens in the Pentagon. And in Moscow there must have been the odd heart attack and some will be cursing my bones though others will be thinking that Lev's got spunk, he's on a roll up there, he must have smuggled a bottle of vodka on board, maybe he'll even switch his engines on in half an hour and return safe and sound.

Not so. The engines were really kaput, and if he'd been testing them for three days and they hadn't sparked it meant something was broken and he should look for a spares shop up there. Lev was furious but he had decided that he didn't want to die angry. He'd known for more than twenty-four hours that he couldn't return, that they were only stringing him along in Baikonur, how could they be so childish if they knew that he knew all the protocols to follow? That's why . . . That's why he knew there was nothing to be done and that he was stymied for good. Following the protocols was the final option the protocols allowed, anything but that. When they read out a protocol to you and tell you to keep calm, it's goodbye. They are talking about a rescue operation. A rescue operation? Do they think I was born yesterday? They knew he had three days left, at the most . . . The bastards, if I knew they were looking at me I'd flash my arse at them through one of these windows.

Lev went off for another sleep. The sun sets every hour, so I'm

125

going to have a nap, he thought. The sleeping pill helped while the spaceship continued circling the earth. Millions of tons of scrap are going around the earth and here's one more, one more going round and round, gift-wrapped present included, he thinks as he falls asleep. They'll find a fine mummy when they stop the ship one day and take a look inside. Some archaeologist in a documentary will explain how I kicked the bucket and maybe the Americans will even turn it into a movie. That's if the K.G.B. doesn't beat them to it, because they'll want to keep it quiet.

The cold woke him up. He didn't think he would feel that so soon. The mechanics had told him that as soon as the engines switch off there are fuel reserves for five days. Three have gone by and there are just two left, then the relentless application of the second law of thermodynamics: everything tends to entropy, the heat from bodies disperses into the void and finally, absolute stillness. Or, in his case, perpetual movement at a constant speed around the earth.

Breakfast, two small packets of dried porridge. After he had eaten them, he went to the wardrobe and put on another sweater and another pair of socks. He would soon be making a return visit. Life is full of surprises, his father forced him to study so he would escape the savage weather of the taiga, and look now, he's going to freeze to death, without snow, ice, blizzards, anything at all; frozen in a perfect vacuum. He will be an eternal monument to Soviet cosmonauts.

Oh, how lucky his father had died three years ago and hadn't had to stomach this tale. Apart from that, no cause for concern – he wasn't married and, even though he knew he had two children with other men's wives – the husbands didn't know and probably never would. He couldn't deny that being a cosmonaut had its advantages, when he went out in Moscow: the best casinos, the best restaurants, the best hotels and the best girls. And, as the secret services were always at his side, he knew it was the safest sex in the world. Once he was talking to a girl and one of his bodyguards came over to tell him her real name and about the venereal disease she had recently contracted. Not forgetting the girls who came out to Baikonur, all medically checked and their clinical histories thoroughly investigated.

The party was over, but he could hardly complain.

He was a young man from a village in the taiga. His father was born and buried there, like his mother, who died a few months after he was born. A brilliant pupil, he had left the village to enter the academy, his teachers had entered him for the examinations and he had passed every one. After that, it was onwards and upwards as they say, and there were only a few flights each year. He couldn't complain. He'd been on six, been given a medal for every single one, prestigious gongs, Crosses of the Russian People, fame and fortune for Captain Lev Riazanov. He lived for his flights, and in the months of training and preparation, he had an even better time of it, the prettiest girls from the whole of Russia at his beck and call . . . And now he had the best view he had ever seen. Only Aldrin and Armstrong, oh and the hapless Uliavnoski, had seen better vistas than he. I really have made it to the top, he reflected, with a smile.

He sat at the controls for a while. The moon was to his left and he had a perfect view of the seas and, through the cameras on board, every minute detail, the shadows the sun spreads over its whole surface.

It is a matt white, as if it had snowed, but with no glare, the opposite of the white of the snow in the taiga. That must have also changed the Americans who made it this far up. They must have assessed them psychologically, no doubt brainwashed them, as soon as they got home, Lev thought. He also had his therapy sessions; it was well known that everyone who had been up above came back in a changed state and needed to be helped to "put their feet back on earth".

It was impossible not to come back a changed man: humanity disappeared, cities disappeared and all there is to see is lots of balls spinning round, the sun, the earth, the moon . . . There must be a typhoon blowing in the Caribbean and how small it seems from up here. And look down there, vanity and more vanity, everything is ephemeral, everything is in a process of departure, all the toil that men do and undo, the generations that come and go. "The philosopher's stone is the absolute void," his beloved Armeniaran liked to say.

Hey, forget all that nonsense and go and see if Ivan has any news . . .

Click.

"Lev?"

"Yes, Ivan, it's me, who the hell do you think it is? Who do you think is up here, Valentina Tereishkova? I haven't got such bad taste, you know!"

"Your shit has really hit the fan, lad, we've got all our ambassadors belly-dancing and giving the lie to your threats. All that rain and weather forecasting . . ."

"So what did they say? Did the C.I.A. get in touch?"

" . . ."

"They must have said something . . . Come on, what did they say?"

"That if you wanted a blanket, they'd deliver you one up there . . ."

"Good, lucky they took it in the right spirit. Ask them if they've still got tachycardia."

"That's enough of that, Lev, and don't hang up on me."

"I'm the one who's hung up, Ivan," he retorted without thinking, and the others didn't laugh.

"We don't know what's wrong. It looks as if the engines have a fault somewhere and that's affected the spare engine, I can't fathom why . . ."

"Come off it, Ivan, I've known for the last two days that I'd be left hanging up here. Quit the play-acting. I could dismantle and reassemble this ship with my eyes shut and if I had a spares shop round the corner I would even dare to pay it a visit and promise to pay on my next trip, but as soon as I had checked out the engine room I knew it was serious. Pack in the play-acting, it doesn't suit you . . ."

"Lev . . ."

"What is it now?"

"I have the President here and he wants to speak to you."

"Tell him the situation is too complicated for me to have to listen to him."

"Lev!"

"Tra-la-la . . ."

"Cosmonaut Lev Riazanov, this is your President speaking . . ."

"Hey, Mr President, the Duma can listen to you, that's what they're paid for."

Click.

At that precise moment, there was a fantastic partial eclipse of the sun; the moon was floating in front of it. He had seen a couple of eclipses up above, but this was something different altogether, he could even see the shadow of the eclipse on the earth, only for a split second but it was so beautiful.

He was looking at the Pleiades, Sagittarius, the Polar Star, and the huge array of stars glittering without a single streetlight to dim them. It was impossible to take in at a single glance. "They are the spirits of dead men," an old woodcutter on the taiga had told him once, "the brightest belong to those who died not long ago and to men of renown, and the constellations are whole families who have reunited up above."

Yes, thought Captain Lev, the whole families up here. Oh, the taiga, that endless spread of trees, those who enter the taiga and don't know the way are lost forever, they can go round and round and never find the way out, how cold it is in the taiga, between beech and fir, pine and larch.

Lev goes to the back of the spaceship, to the medicine chest.

"Perfect!" he exclaimed. There were enough sleeping pills to put a whole crew to sleep for a year. Pain was all that Captain Lev Riazanov feared. He had never thought about it seriously, it had never crossed his mind; if he had to, he would, end of story. He knew that as a general rule cosmonauts didn't suffer pain when they died – they either pegged out at the beginning or the end. And it all happened so quickly that they generally didn't suffer, but this was something else. Obviously, it was very different up there and the prospect of freezing to death was hardly congenial.

He planned it all. He would sit on the control bridge, opposite the main window, would wrap himself up well and take the sleeping pills. He would not wake up. Before the effect of the pills wore off, the temperature in the spaceship would sink to thirty degrees below zero and he would have passed on. He had never liked leaving anything to chance so he began to pile clothing around the bridge, space overalls and spare and emergency equipment. There wasn't that much as it was a solo flight. He grabbed the tube of sleeping pills and put it next to his seat. The ship's energy supply would run out in three to four hours, three to four hours to feel the ship was cooling down. He had everything he wanted.

"Lev . . ." His voice was sombre.

"I see we are on the same wavelength. That's wonderful. If it's possible, if this can goes round and round for years, I'd like you to push me into outer space, like Uliavnoski, rather than being burned up returning into the atmosphere. And, as it's time for special requests, it would be fantastic to be sent to the sun, don't you reckon, Ivan? Captain

Lev Riazanov, the first man to reach the sun. Millions of photons would come to the earth knowing how to speak Russian. That's all."

"Lev, wait—"

Click.

Captain Lev Riazanov dissolved the pills in a small bottle of water. He sat on the seat on the bridge and wrapped himself in all the clothing and bedding, put T-shirts over his legs and thicker items on top. He didn't want the cold to wake him up too soon.

He started drinking the liquid from the bottle and relaxed, breathed slowly, the second law of thermodynamics, bodies lose heat, heat disperses . . . "No, Mr Riazanov," Professor Armeniaran would have told him, "you aren't losing heat, it's the universe that is gaining heat." Captain Lev Riazanov was falling asleep, was breathing slowly, they had taught him to inhale very gradually in the Academy so as not to be nervous at take-off. Now he could see the sun coming out, now it was the moon and the earth, he could even see the taiga, he thought, I'm lost in the taiga; he was falling asleep.

"It's very cold and I'm going to freeze. Isn't it great to be home?"

THE SONSOVABITCH!

On 9 November, 1989, an astonished Joseph B. Newman was watching his television as some brutes dared climb right onto the top of the wall. The Berlin Wall. Astonished is putting it mildly, and a super-superlative of astonished would be too. What did that mean exactly? It meant the whole thing was fucked. Precisely.

If they pricked him, they wouldn't find any blood. All the same, he felt a little queasy.

After the brutes, after the toasts of champagne and beer, came the politicians' speeches. The news lasted a good long time, long enough for him to be sure he wasn't dreaming, for him to believe his eyes.

Over ten years ago he had given up some of the routine rituals that had governed his life, but, disciplined as he was, not the post-midnight ritual of sitting next to his window, book in hand, under the light in the corner of his dining room. What would he read tonight? Whatever he fancied, and he'd take his time: for twenty-seven years he'd only read with one eye. He would park the other one outside, waiting for someone to appear in Peony Park or along Roberts . . . He was sick of all that!

"Sonsovabitch! Sonsovabitch!" he exclaimed in Russian. He hadn't shouted like that from the day he arrived in Omaha in 1960.

Every five seconds, while he couldn't read the book he'd opened out of inertia, his brain kept repeating, bawling, though his cries in perfect Russian never left the inside of his skull: Sonsovabitch!

So then . . . What Reagan said was for real, he'd done them in . . . It wasn't just propaganda . . . All that time putting up with Hollywood, the *New York Times* and eating hamburgers, always imagining the world would recognise the superiority of the U.S.S.R. any moment now . . . And American football, and Mark Spitz and the Celtics against the Lakers, and every record by Aretha Franklin . . . The sonsovabitch had forgotten him!

He got up from his armchair and threw his book at the wall, went into the street and didn't look to see whether anyone was coming. Or whether there was a note under the mat or in the branches of the plants along the side of the garden, or even whether a car was revving up and making an escape. The sonsovabitch, all those years spent expecting to cop it in his supermarket trolley or a black eye when he was paying at the checkout . . . All those years spent reading the letters he received from back to front in case there was some codeword to alert him . . . the sonsovabitch . . . All those years spent observing the guy in the petrol station, who seemed a likely contact; the local doctor's secretary; the gas man, the water man and the electricity man and every sonovabitch under the sun . . . All those years spent waiting on the riverbank, on distant benches, on little used bridges, as if going to such places might herald the arrival of his contact and, through his contact, the start of a mission.

It was incredible, incredible, downright incredible, the sonsovabitch . . .

So it was all for real and the Wall was as flimsy as rice paper. And Joseph B. Newman could go to fucking hell! To fucking hell along with his beard, that had itched him from day one. "He'll get used to it," they told the K.G.B. Like hell he had, it had itched forever, and in summer, drove him mad. Joseph B. Newman could go to hell with the whole of his family tree and the dates for every single branch . . . It was a fucking joke, and even he could see the funny side, what a fucking . . . Just incredible.

Seventy-one years old. He was no age to do a James Bond. No age and no desire either, that lot could take a running jump . . . The sonsovabitch . . . He should go to the C.I.A. Absolutely! He felt like going to the C.I.A. and telling them that he was really Dimitri Batiuchov, from Voronezh, that he had left his wife and two daughters to train in the art of espionage, converted by the grace of Communism. The sonsovabitch. Ha! And Gorbachev signing the Nuclear Arms Treaty and even handing over Siberia and ready to continue with the sale of Alaska, if necessary . . .

Twenty-nine years hiding from intelligence services who can't even have known of his existence. Or perhaps they had, perhaps they knew everything, absolutely everything. And as they knew, they had left him out on a limb, he didn't bother them in the slightest. A sleeper, a sleeper . . . A goddam sleeper . . . A forgotten man! And what was in it for him if he told them? Agh! They'd piss themselves laughing, take him to the Metropolitan Museum of Art and out him in the presence of all those exhibits that had been brought from all around the world, like just another exotic trophy. The C.I.A. must be pissing themselves laughing: "Oh, Batiuchov, that fool who reckons he'll get a summons to the Pentagon and has yet to cotton on that Moscow has totally forgotten him, ho ho ho . . ." Taking precautions all that time and now he couldn't get those brutes jumping up and down on top of the Wall out of his head.

Batiuchov fell asleep as he did on so many nights, with a drop of vodka. Only a little drop, enough for him to feel how heavy his head was, enough to need a pillow to rest it on.

The morning after, when he woke up, he tried to see things differently, what could he do? He tried not to listen to the radio. He didn't switch on the television and, when he went out, he looked at his mailbox as anxiously as he looked a few minutes later at the faces of passers-by to see – anything was possible in the new situation – if one of those faces was signalling to him, a grimace, maybe that car that had been parked in the same spot for two days, maybe . . .

More maybes: maybe it was all one big diversion and, in fact, the fall of the Wall was simply a simulation, was all pre-planned, the action was about to begin and the Soviet bloc was preparing its definitive assault. Maybe . . .

РОДИНА-МАТЬ
ЗОВЕТ!

ПОЧТА СССР

ALEKSANDR VOLKOV

Aleksandr Volkov (Bogorodsk, 1914 – Nizhny Novgorod, 1982) was a teacher in the agricultural collective in his village of birth for forty years. He spent his whole life in the collective, except for the interlude of the Second World War. His memoir, A Farm in Moscow, was published in 1965. He was both a committed socialist and a critic of the regime and had numerous problems as a result of one of the stories we have included here, "The Russian Road", which first appeared in the collective's magazine. The debate over Volkov's change of attitude has been central to the understanding of the evolution of Russian literature in the twentieth century. Was it a change of attitude or a premeditated stance? Gradualism? Pragmatism? Resistance? Volkov managed to achieve a school for the collective after providing the Party with a fake memoir. His now celebrated saying, "I am changing my past for your future", became the school's motto. The authorities never rumbled its real meaning.

It has still not been possible to bring out a definitive edition of his collected short stories because of his multiple heteronyms and the varied nature of their styles, themes and dates. Volkov's first stories are full of irony, even sarcasm. "The Russian Road", published in 1936, is a good example. "The Worker and the Farm Girl" was the first story he published after he returned from Germany in 1946. "The War against the Voromians" is his last story, written after one of his children – he had thirteen – came back from military service in Chechnya. Volkov stated he was unable to finish it.

THE WORKER AND THE FARM GIRL

*The world rests on a huge pillow woven from the skin
and sinews of women*

Ukrainian proverb

I will tell this story just as I remember it.

I have thought about it so often my memory of it is rather confused.
The events that change us also seem to change the places and times
when they happened. I have thought so hard about all this I feel I can
only remember fragments, that I have refashioned my memory to such
an extent I no longer remember what I really experienced. Nevertheless,
I do remember it, I really do.

I will start with Maxim.

The moment he returned, he had all kinds of feet made. For driving
tractors, for tilling the soil, for walking through mud and snow, and
yet more for going out at night and partying. His stumps had healed
well.

The prosthetics from the military hospital had worked, and the
collective's cobbler and carpenter had provided the wonderful final
touches. Prosthetics enabled him to stand without hardly ever tiring; he
had even once raced for a wager, but best of all he didn't need a wheel-
chair or crutches. The medical reports noted his back was as strong

as ever, and his spine was healthy, curved from the side and straight as seen from the front: it was perfect, neither the prosthetics nor the hours he spent driving tractors and caterpillars, excavators and lorries affected the position of his pelvis or vertebra.

As soon as he finished the day's work, he went straight to the swimming pool and gymnasium. First he swam three kilometres, faster than many strong, healthy men. Then, he would work out on the horse. Before the war he had worked a lot on the rings, but when he returned he chose the horse, because with the horse, where his feet had got in the way, now he could leave his prosthetics on the floor and let his arms go through their paces with various whirls and jumps. The exercise made him feel good because although he worked long hours, he was always sitting down, driving tractors or lorries, transporting one thing or another. It wasn't like before when he was a mechanic and spent the whole day going to and fro. He was the first up. When everyone was still asleep, Maxim Salingerev was inspecting oil, water and fuel levels, and after greasing axles and bearings, he would start up the tractor or caterpillar. If it was harvest time, he spent longer than anyone on the harvester, if it was the ploughing season, when it was necessary to drive the lorries long distances, he came top of every list, once more the example to follow.

When she learned that Maxim was returning with the others, Maria Esmerz, my best friend, became very anxious. She found it hard to sleep at night, she ate too little today and too much tomorrow and from time to time took a break in order to slow down her breathing, scold me, cry or kiss and hug me.

The grannies had selected her from all the girls on the collective farm to sing in front of the returning soldiers. The boys had been away for more than five years and the old women thought it would be a good idea to put on a party that reminded them of life before they left. None of the mothers and grannies had been able to forget the day when their boys had climbed into the lorries to go off to the front. For their return, the grannies had decided, Maria Esmerz should be the one to sing once again. Some hadn't seen their boys since then and the memory of that last meal was etched on everyone's minds, as was the speech by the director, the dancing, the singing and the farewell song that Maria Esmerz sang that made more than one cry. The grandads took responsibility for the meal and the grannies for the welcome home party, which also welcomed many soldiers who had been demobbed the year before, like Maria's father or mine.

The minute Maria discovered the men were coming home, she got bellyache. And it ached even more when she read the list of those coming and saw that Maxim was due to be on the bus bringing them back to the farm. She said nothing, nobody needed to do anything, best keep quiet about these things; we women know how they end up affecting us.

She had to sing for the soldiers, for everyone, but she realised that nothing would be like last time. My God, that last time! She was only twelve then! And they had had to help her dress up and do her plaits, and she was the girl who was dying to be the centre of the party . . . And they'd even had to tell her to get off the stage because she didn't want to stop and sang two more songs than planned . . . When she recalled that, or when we pulled her leg ("Maria, this time don't whirl round so quickly, your dress will ride up too high and you're not a little girl anymore . . .", "Maria, perhaps best not sing the one about the love-struck wolf this time . . .") she would put her butter-making tools down, calmly wash her hands and say she had to go back to the lavatory.

"Enough! That's enough of that! I need to go for another pee!"

And then we laughed. I remember it as if it were yesterday. You wouldn't be yourself if you forgot certain things.

All the old folk, the young kids and the women from the collective, the boys and girls . . . We all waited almost two hours for the bus to arrive. Our hairdos looked smart, we smelled sweet and were wearing our party clothes. We girls wore skirts and clogs and necklaces made from herbs the oldest used to bring happiness and fertility. We'd been buttering our faces for a month before going to sleep and the previous day had washed each other's hair with homemade soap and camomile water. We looked gorgeous.

The weeks before the men returned had been frantic, everybody had had to work longer hours, we wanted the collective to be clean, and to be able to take a rest for a couple of days. The cows' stables were clean and we had given them enough forage not to have worry about them. The sheep pens as well. The milk tanks were clean and empty, tractors and caterpillars and carts as well, and the houses whitewashed. We were exhausted. We felt so fed up on the days up to their return that we kept saying: "If they don't like it, they can go back where they come from."

We were right in the front. Maria had to go for a pee twice she was so nervous. She kept looking to see if anyone was coming and asking me if I could hear anything and then she would run back to the lavatory for a pee and belted it back. "Do I look pretty? Do you mean that or are you just being polite? What about my hair? I should have made plaits, my mother said it was too forward not to wear plaits." She made me feel nervous and I had to go for a pee too.

Finally, the bus drove into sight at the end of the road. We were right in the front and behind us, our mothers and the youngsters who were too young to go to war or the factories, the soldiers who'd already been discharged, and the women in mourning, who already knew their sons wouldn't be arriving in that bus or any other. We swayed, surged forward, the boys behind shoved their mothers, and their sisters advanced a few metres, then came back to the group until the bus stopped in front of us.

I remember it as if it were yesterday, as if I was seeing it right now, how he came down the steps on crutches, needing no help from anyone, he'd always been very strong, and I remember how he looked at everyone, almost intimidating us. As if to say, I don't want any of your pity, what happened, happened. And I heard him, when everyone was hugging, shouting for joy, crying, Maxim simply said, "Hello, Maria," and that was that . . . And that was that! I saw how Maria was rooted to the spot and speechless. She knew he had lost his feet and knew he was recovering, though from comments made in letters other boys sent their mothers, not from him, he'd not written to her in a long time . . . At that point, Maria turned round, gave me a hug and burst into tears.

She hadn't seen him for almost six years, since 8 June, 1940.

That day was two days before Maria's thirteenth birthday. After we finished the dances our grannies had taught us from childhood, the traditional dances to celebrate sowing, ripening and the harvest, she walked up onto the stage.

Everybody said she ought to go to Moscow and have proper singing lessons, but she replied that she wanted to marry on the collective farm, that the boys weren't as clever in Moscow. She was always a bit outlandish. She climbed onto the stage and started to sing. The grannies and even the men were all crying. I can still see her, swirling round, her flaxen hair flying as the song described the ears of wheat swaying in the wind, or as her feet flew across the boards. Afterwards, mothers danced with their sons and fathers with their daughters, grandads with granddaughters, everyone in step to the sound from the collective's record player. There was a tremendous din, and the men smoked endlessly and drank vodka.

Maria made me accompany her to the table where Maxim was

sitting. She didn't dare go by herself, but the second we got there – before twice deciding to go for a pee – I ran off and left them by themselves. I've described the scene to myself so often I can really tell it as it was, "Maxim, Maxim . . . I'm . . ."

"What's wrong, Maria? You sang beautifully, you should go to Moscow and see if they want you at the opera house. Know what I think? You'd do better than most girls who—"

"Yes, Maxim, I wanted . . ."

"No, you were really very good and—"

"Shush, Maxim, don't you see we've not much time?" She told me – and certainly she had the character to do it – that she'd told him to shut up. Poor Maxim must have been astonished.

"So, what's wrong, Maria?"

"I want you to write to me from the front, I promise to reply to every letter as soon as they arrive, I will, Maxim, I will reply to every single one, long letters to cheer you up, you will write, Maxim, won't you? Promise?"

"Maria, I think . . ."

"Please, Maxim, I want you to write to me."

"Alright, but I must ask your parents, Maria, you're very young." She always says she has never hated anything as much as that moment when he said she was too young.

"I've already told them 'a lie' and they say they will be only too happy to get your news." Your news! "Your news," she says she said, she never used that word, what a joke! "You know my parents regard you highly. My father will be leaving with you. He'll tell you one of these days. Maxim, you will write, won't you? I won't tell anyone what you say, I won't, Maxim, I promise."

"Alright, Maria, alright, I'll write, though I don't know if I'll be able to very often . . ."

And I watched as the table filled up with boys who were off to enlist in the morning and Maria returned to our group.

I also remember the other occasion when she went to sing to a group of soldiers. She asked me to accompany her to the neighbouring collective farm. It must have been in 1944 and a group of wounded soldiers had returned to convalesce at home. The things we saw there . . .

People kept saying the war was coming to an end but the end never seemed in sight. We had made our homes at a time when, wherever you looked, in front, behind, this side and that, war was all there was . . . I didn't leave the dressing room until she did. Other girls and boys had come out to dance and sing first in honour of the returning soldiers, and I stayed behind the curtains. From there I could see a very sad sight: she was up on the stage and the soldiers were sat on chairs, bandaged, one missing an arm, another both legs, another blind, all the war-wounded, crippled for life. She was singing without a single spotlight to shine on her and light her up as she sang the saddest song. In the war years, we fought a different battle on the farm, the daily set-to, the long, exhausting hours. The grimness of the front reached the collective in the form of a trickle of dead and crippled. In addition to the absence of men and accumulated tiredness we had the extra demands imposed from above. They requested we increased production – our area hadn't been affected by the advancing German troops and the front and cities under siege were in need of powdered milk.

Innovations came and went but our lives kept on at the same pace. Engineers came and installed machines for making cream cheese, dehydrators to produce powdered milk and churns that produced butter faster. Our farm was one of the most productive, and from time to time letters arrived urging us to produce even more milk, and even more, and posters with little boys and girls drinking milk, and others exhorting us to resist; we women were the warriors' pillows, they said. There were posters everywhere: "Women supporting the front", "Women, your husbands need you", "Food for the front", "Heroes and heroines of Russia", etc. Whenever an engineer came to check how the machinery was going, he would bring us a stack.

We worked long, exhausting hours and our morale was often almost at rock bottom until we finally received the news that the army's advance had been halted by the onset of winter. From then on, every day seemed slightly better and the burden of work lighter. There was a feeling of sisterhood that is difficult to define. Our work brought us together. At night our teachers made up the hours we were missing by not attending school.

We were exhausted, but we also knew it was that or nothing, and the visits from men on leave from the front lines made that clear enough. Nevertheless, life went on: war taught us all that life never stops.

I learned more from Maria than from the war.

It was the second year, around September 1942. In the first two years there were days when she was blissful and others when she looked downcast, and others when she seemed even more downcast, and then I would see her with a broad smile on her face. She never said a word until one day she couldn't keep it secret anymore. She ushered me into her bedroom and told me she was going to show me what she called her treasures. As I walked in, I saw that she had a big poster hanging above the end of her bed.

It was one that had disappeared from our meeting room. The poster was based on the monument from the Paris Exhibition: the statue of *Rabochiy i Kolkhoznitsa*, "The Worker and the Farm Girl", raising the hammer and sickle. In red letters it said "United forever we shall never be defeated". She also showed me a figurine, a bronze reproduction of the couple in the poster. She had bought it from one of the engineers who serviced the butter churns. She had wrapped a sheet around the shiny figurine and at night she placed it between the mattress and the wall and fell asleep gazing at it.

She extracted a sheaf of forty or fifty letters from under the blankets.

"I sleep with them," she said, "I hug them and go to sleep."

As I watched her singing to the soldiers, I kept thinking about the letters, the statue and the poster. More than five years separated the two most important parties we have ever held on the farm, for the departure and return of the soldiers. In the meantime: the letters, the worker and the farm girl.

It had never struck me before, but when Maxim returned, I saw that he was a lot like the worker in the monument. And the boy who'd left the farm couldn't bear to see himself looking as he did, and that's why the doctors were still making new prosthetics for him.

The increasingly frequent correspondence between Maria and Maxim suddenly stopped at the beginning of 1945. Maxim knew from the letters he received that she was sleeping with his letters, and knew of the existence of the statue and poster. Far away, Maria grew up as the years of war passed.

The days after the soldiers' return were the worst we ever experienced on the farm. Worse even than when the epidemic killed our cows or that mysterious disease hit the forage.

I had never seen everyone look so terrified. You had to be careful what you said and how you said it, everyone was so on edge they quarrelled all the time. People were so nervy! Those of us who were more even-tempered tried to keep the peace. Some of us women and girls had even talked about it and would appear when necessary to calm emotions; the second someone gave a shout, five of six or us would appear to cool the situation.

The men's return upset everyone. It was necessary to reorganise everything, share out the work among families and also give jobs to the cripples and war-wounded. They tried to give the blind tasks that didn't require sight like cutting paper and wrapping up cheese. One fellow only had one arm and was assigned to paint the cows' stables with anti-rust paint. And there were others who had lost the work habit, who had to get rid of the crutches they carried in their heads . . . It was about getting everyone back to work.

We wanted it to be like it was before the war; that was why life had to carry on when the men returned home. After the first two months, months of changes and upheaval, everyone had set tasks once again. Their return allowed us to work shorter days and gradually everything settled down. Everyone helped, work was even found for the worst cases, men in wheelchairs who took over the accounts, the deaf who worked on machines that weren't dangerous . . .

There were exceptional cases like Maxim's. Maxim couldn't return to the repair-shops, but after a week of trial runs he was soon driving all kinds of vehicles. The doctors and the cobbler kept re-adapting the prosthetics.

Now, in retrospect, I think how that was all quite normal. The men returning home had to take back the positions we had filled and had to get used to working again and, in many cases, to doing different jobs and learning new ones, because a lot of new machinery had been installed during the war. Seen like that I realise it all required time, that the earthquake we had endured for six years had left many fractures that would need time to heal.

They were very hard months. We all made an effort so that the newcomers felt like working again and kept to their timetables; the quicker we could restore shifts, the daily round of chores, the tiredness at the end of the day, the sooner we would shake off the nightmare of the war. And they needed that more than we did. That's why alcohol was banned from the whole collective farm, that's why they imposed strict timetables, that's why we all had to try to be a little more considerate to others: the war was a gale that had bared our souls to fire and ice. The collective farm was all we had, the only thing that could help us.

If everything else gradually fell into place, Maxim was a special case. He had an iron will, but others soon followed his example – everyone had to get used to a situation of order and calm. There were problems and tensions but nothing comparable to wartime. Even so, when they asked someone whether he could tackle a task he had never done, it was with the utmost patience. The crippled had experienced unimaginable horrors, but time makes the lame walk and the blind see ...

Were there problems? Lots. All we could ever want, more than we could cope with. The sisterhood of wartime gave way to quarrels, but that also meant everything was settling back into place. Earthquakes don't last a lifetime.

And what about me? I was bearing up, and Maria was teetering along, as if she were walking on the edge of an unknown precipice and I tried to keep her company. In the first months after the soldiers' return she was either in tears or angry: there was no halfway station. I sometimes saw her crying, and when I said something to console her, she flew into a rage, and sometimes we quarrelled because she was unbearable and the upshot was never-ending tears. The milk churns hit the ground more loudly when she lifted them down, and the levers and machine went more quickly, everything seemed harder and tougher, and the machines more fast and furious.

We couldn't talk about anything that might relate to Maxim. About the swimming pool, the workshops, the tractors or the work the tractors were doing. She even once let drop that we were better off during the war, that now everything was upside down, the men were drunken layabouts and they'd all caught the clap. When she'd said it, she would burst into tears, and the more drastic her declarations, the more she cried.

I'm thinking back to the day when I saw her look her saddest. That was the day she didn't even get angry when she found something misplaced, she simply picked it up and put it right. She acted similarly if the grease jammed the gears in the engines too frequently, and with all the other little hassles of the day that would usually send her into a rage. She worked like a robot, saying nothing, as if she were a machine that was only waiting for the siren and the end of the working day. She said virtually nothing the whole morning, "Yes", "No", "I've finished", little else.

It was then that I heard her scream. I ran to where she was working, and saw her there, half stretched out over the butter vat with her arm inside. A blade of the revolving screw had caught her arm and spun her round. It kept turning round and stirring the cream, but luckily her arm had got stuck in the butter on the sides, trapped in thick layers of grease. I stopped the machine and other women rushed over.

We carried her to hospital. The doctors said her arm was in a very bad state, broken bones, dislocation, torn muscles and ligaments. And she had been lucky, we were all thinking, because it was only her arm, the screw could have dragged her whole body into the vat. In order to carry her, we had covered her up, we couldn't bear to look at that dangling arm – turned purple because of the wrench – luckily the farm doctor could give her an anaesthetic. When I remember, when I think how I found her, when I think how the screw bent her over the vat, I get the shivers.

Maria went to and from hospital for seven months. She would tell us that when they had finished sewing her up on one side they would start cutting her open on the other, or vice versa. "They make me a new sleeve every time," she'd say. When we asked her how it had happened, she always replied she had slipped on a piece of butter and that her arm had got trapped inside the vat. Bad luck, she'd add.

I kept her company in the weeks they allowed her to return home. The director had given me permission to stay and look after her for a few hours, so her parents could go to work knowing there was someone at home with her. We had visitors and went for walks in the fields. The operations were successful, though she knew right from the start she would never recover full mobility and that her arm would always dangle down rather awkwardly. She even recovered her good temper from way back.

Maxim came to see her five or six times, but she acted as coldly as she could. He made a very loud noise coming up the stairs. His wooden feet pounded as if a giant were approaching. He sat next to us, and when I acted as if I were about to leave, they both asked me to stay. If the silence was unbearable and the conversation became stupid and meaningless, ridiculous exchanges about the weather or the farm, I didn't even try to hide how annoyed I felt. Luckily Maxim noticed and left before I exploded.

Maria gradually began to move her arm again although it never fell to match the other and she could never lift it as high. It was her right arm, but as soon as Maria felt like working again, carrying out a task or two, the director found us a job taking the cows to the milking parlour, and that was very relaxing, as if the cows were grazing. I seemed destined to accompany her in all her tasks until she felt strong or brave enough not to need anyone. She was happy and only seemed angry when she saw Maxim drive past in a lorry or tractor.

Ah. Maxim.

It all kicked off again one day when we were a long way from the farm. The cows always went where the grass was greenest, that is, the further from the milking-hose the better. As soon as we had led them a suitable distance, they went off by themselves. The sun was setting and Maxim asked if we wanted to ride on his trailer, that he would take us to the farm, and I was just about to say yes when I felt my arm being squeezed in a place that still hurts. "No, thanks, Maxim, we'd prefer to walk back." What could I say without risking Maria's anger . . .

She avoided meeting him, but no day went by when, despite the farm being so large, she didn't bump into him five or six times. And he looked out for her and always found an excuse to drive by the milking parlour. He had to pass her section to fill his tank, get a spare part or sign receipts. The other road was shorter if he had to see his boss, but he always chose the route that went past the milking parlour and the precinct where the cows were kept. The other girls would laugh and joke, and I would too.

"He's back again, he's back."

"That's the sixth time today."

But she kept to her stubborn pose, never said a word to him, sealed her lips and acted as if no-one was passing by.

It seemed like a perpetual stalemate. To be frank, I was sick to death of that business. I had started courting with Piotr and had my own quarrels and reconciliations to negotiate.

It was a day when we were changing in the dressing rooms in the milking parlour. Maria had a red blotch on her arm, and when I asked her what it was she said it wasn't anything to worry about, that it came and went without rhyme or reason. But the fact is the blotch was very big, and luckily we were in time, because Maria's arm had a very dangerous infection. If we hadn't been, they would have had to amputate her forearm.

The treatment lasted quite a long time, the fever from her infection came and went, but she couldn't work, needed complete rest. I kept her company, her parents trusted me blindly. She sometimes slept the whole morning, sometimes the whole afternoon. I moved in to live with them so I could look after the house as well as her. The medication started to have an effect, but the weeks went by and she was still very drowsy. I tried to cheer her up, said she looked like a princess in bed, so white and frail, a romantic heroine, and she said that when she saw Piotr she would tell him I was a horrible harpy.

We had few visitors. Maxim would drop by a couple of times a week, but as far as Maria was concerned, it was as if we were alone. She had taken down the poster and hidden the statue the day Maxim returned and, by hiding her wartime past she seemed able to forget how much she had loved him and how much she had suffered.

However, one morning, when Maria was asleep, everything changed. I was looking for linen to remake her bed. I hurt myself. I put my hand in among the sheets and broke a nail, I had knocked it against the arm or the scythe of Mukhina's monument, and, lo and behold, behind the sheets lay the key to this whole story. Maria was asleep, and I proceeded carefully so as not to wake her. I took out the sheets and the statue with them. Poor Maria. She had put a bandage around the Worker's feet, neatly enough, and he now looked like a giant, a colossus with feet of clay. The farm girl was still holding the scythe next to the worker's hammer, but her arm was now slightly twisted, bent slightly backwards, just as Maria's was when she lifted it and tried to touch the tips of her fingers on her other hand.

Maxim came the next morning; Maria was asleep. I went out on to the stairs and told him to be as quiet as he could. I showed him what I had found.

"Look, that belongs to Maria, she kept it here all these years, she bought it during the war," I told him as I put the rug under his feet and he walked into the room.

Maxim sat by the bed, with the bronze statue resting on his legs.

I shut the door and left, left them alone.

The rest is the happy ending we all wanted.

The war left millions of dead and wounded and hundreds of towns and cities destroyed, but I can truly say that what I remember most is the story of Maxim and Maria, more so even than what happened in my own life. Our future doesn't belong to us, and I fear our past doesn't either.

I know where this memory derives its strength; the things that are really true are made with love. But I don't know what lay behind it, because I never dared ask her what she was doing standing next to the butter vat. Because I never dared ask her why she put her arm there.

I haven't a clue what happened. It must have been the war that drove us all crazy.

THE RUSSIAN ROAD

The immense steppe is divided down the middle by a road that gets smaller and smaller to the point when it disappears. A man is walking between the puddles many *versts* away. It is Akaki Sergueyevitch.

He is advancing imperceptibly because he is a long way away and seems tiny, growing very slowly as he walks from one side of the path to the other looking for less muddy stretches. When he sees the road is bone dry, he proceeds, puffs his chest out and looks ahead until he suddenly slips and is back dodging puddles. He is whistling the tune of one of the songs the revolutionaries were singing in the city. He is wearing a new overcoat, like the one his grandfather always said he wanted to buy, and boots that are too big and splattered with mud to the ankles. He is carrying his gun over his shoulder and the strap runs across his chest. He makes slow progress because he is feeling weak, he has been on the road for two days and has eaten next to nothing since yesterday morning, those blasted peasants refused to give him more than a mouthful of dry bread, and that was after he had told them that the revolution had triumphed:

"So the revolution has triumphed, has it? Right then, where are the trucks full of food and clothing? And what about electricity? Where is the electricity?" shouted the women of the town he had crossed as they threw handfuls of mud at him to scare him away.

Ah, those women are just ignorant, thinks Akaki Sergueyevitch. It's not right. We've just carried through the revolution, changed the world and they chase me out of town like a stray dog. And those animals have left my coat dirtier than a pile of dung. Ah, those peasants are just ignorant, he rasps angrily.

Akaki thinks the road seems even longer, his boots are giving his feet blisters and he feels hungrier and hungrier – those foul bitches gave me nothing. It is still a few *versts* to his town, and that's why he sticks at it as best he can, but he is so hungry and so weak! He has been making the revolution for a whole year from city to city and has never ever been so hungry. Everybody spoke of collectivising but, as usual, spoke about collectivising what wasn't theirs. As soon as people had something to sell, they went to sell it on the black market. Speculators! There was no way you could get a decent hot meal except by deciding to hoard and act like a capitalist! They really made him angry sometimes! However did they expect the revolution to triumph, if when you asked for a salted sardine it cost you two roubles and into the bargain they made faces that would frighten any witch away!

Ah! And what about the civil servants? The civil servants? His grandfather had already suffered at their hands when he went to the city to work with them and now they'd not even given him bread coupons to take home, the revolution wins and they didn't even give you bread coupons. The Party had said, the train is free . . . So everyone gets on the train! Of course, it's free! Now and then you see Akaki kick the ground, he is very, very angry and so hungry he could eat a horse. Good, that's one stretch less to go.

Ah! Perhaps his luck is in. At the point when the road disappears, he sees a shape in the distance that's approaching quickly: it may be a horse. Maybe they have come to look for him and couldn't find him. Someone must have warned them he was coming, and as they didn't know which road he would take, they had gone out in all directions. Ah, how happy he now feels, they'll ride him into town on horseback! That must be it. How wonderful. Akaki lifts his arms, waves them and jumps as he splashes in the mud. It has almost reached him.

The horse has stopped galloping, but is still trotting briskly. It is a magnificent steed, the like of which he's not seen for a long time. I thought they had eaten them all during the revolution and that none as tall, strong and handsome as this were left, he thinks. Wonderful, its rider will dismount and lead the horse by the reins so I can ride in to town. The whole town must be expecting me, even the lovely Natasha – he had even stopped thinking about her – even the lovely Natasha must be expecting me. Of course, the letters I wrote her must have set her heart on fire and she must have heard I was coming and you can be sure she will be there, to the fore of all the other women, he thinks.

As soon as he is level with Akaki, the rider brings his horse to a canter, but doesn't bother to stop. Ah, it's poor Akaki back from making the revolution. What a sight, splattered in mud from head to toe, the rider thinks, gesturing scornfully, and, without saying a single word, he spurs his horse back into a gallop. The animal throws up so much sludge it muddies Akaki Sergueyevitch's overcoat all over again.

"Go to hell, Baron de Berezinov, go to hell, you and your horse, I hope you fall and break your damned neck!" he shouts as loudly as he can, when the rider is far away and can't hear him. I don't believe it, it's the Baron de Berezinov, still alive, wasn't the revolution supposed to put an end to the nobility? Well, looks like someone hasn't done his job properly, and what a horse he was riding, white, beautiful, splattered with mud but still as strong as when it left the stable, the baron's horse has clearly not gone hungry!

Akaki blushes slightly when he thinks how amazed he was to see the horse trot past. The baron must have had a good laugh, seeing him splattered from head to toe, and on foot, with not even an old nag to bring him home.

And, he reasoned, I said nothing because I was so shocked to see him that, for a moment, I thought it must be the baron's ghost wandering this land after the townsfolk chopped his head off, because that's what they should have done, though the poor people in town have been so terrorised by the baron for so many years that they can't have dared. As soon as I get there, I will establish a revolutionary committee and I will go and arrest the baron in his castle, I will, I will, and put his head on the block and goodbye, baron. We will turn the castle into the Party headquarters, and they will be so happy in Moscow that you can bet they'll make me district head, when I inform them that we have a castle for Party headquarters and land to make a collective farm. And Natasha, I bet Natasha will be there to welcome me on the outskirts of town and she will be the wife of Akaki Sergueyevitch, the future district head.

And Akaki walks on along the path. He is as hungry as a wolf, but it's not very far now, in fact, you can see the smoke from the bakery and the forge, the two plumes of smoke that mark out the town in calm weather. His eyes cloud over. Oh, I so want to be back home, Akaki thinks, one whole year making the revolution and not sleeping on my bed at home, not eating the potatoes my mother cooks, not seeing my friends Sacha, Ivan and Vladimir, oh, oh, wonderful, they must all be waiting for me in the square.

Akaki speeds up. His feet are hurting and it is hot, the sweat's pouring down, but now he is almost there he walks faster and faster. Oh, these peasants are so sly, none to be seen anywhere, they must all be in the centre, hiding away to give him a big welcome, they're so . . . But the fact is when he passes the first houses he only sees three old dears who are sitting against a wall in the sun as they pod beans.

"Look, there's a soldier," one says.

"And look how filthy he is, his face is black with mud, what can he want now?"

"They like war, but not work . . . Revolution! He's a good for nothing . . . look how dirty he is," says the third.

Akaki acts as if he has heard nothing and walks on. Well, well, the eternal ignorance of a backward people, that's all there is to it, he'll have a hard time being the standard bearer for the revolution in Prokopov, but fine, he gives his face a wash – it's black with mud and sweat – and strides firmly towards the centre of town.

The usual people are there and Akaki now feels he is returning home and is filled with nostalgia . . . He has seen so many towns and cities, he has seen so many squares and streets, huge, grandiose cities, squares full of theatres and academies . . . But the square in Prokopov is his, and he can see the church, and the smithy, and the bakery, and when he stands in the centre of the square, he wants to cry, and the mud under his feet is the same he used to slide on when he was a child, running from one side of the square to the other, and the same old sun lights up the front of the church and the gilded panels of the dome, oh, how he had been longing for home, he really does want to cry, though he can't, because he is a revolutionary soldier. Akaki Sergueyevitch from Prokopov. And look, there's no school, oh, how barbaric, how backward! How backward! The place is so backward, how do they ever expect to get electricity?

Some men come over to him but don't recognise him.

"What have you come to Prokopov for, soldier?" one asks.

"Are there troops nearby, soldier, or have you come by yourself?" asks another. He keeps quiet but then he decides to speak.

"No, peasants of Prokopov. I have come by myself."

"Oh." The peasants are astonished; the soldier must be from the village, he has the same accent as they have when he pronounces the last "o" of Prokopov. "You say he's not from here, but, he must be, he can't be from Kontrakopov, they pronounce it Prokopov. Well, if he's from here, it must be, what was the name of that lad, you know, the one we sent to the revolution, you, you know, it must be Akaki Sergueyevitch."

"Yes, peasants, it's me, I am Akaki Sergueyevitch, the soldier who represented Prokopov in the revolution and made sure the name of our village echoed as one that contributed to the freedom and solidarity of the working-class peoples, we who must give a lead to the workers of the world to—"

"He's such a good speaker," the peasants remark as Akaki Sergueyevitch raises his voice. Akaki repeats the sentences he heard in all those speeches, emphasising the passages that underline the meaning of this declaration or that. Peasants fill the square, surround Akaki and listen for what he will say next.

He talks the way he saw his companions on the committee talk, waving his hands and addressing the villagers, looking into their eyes. While the peasants mutter, "Yes, you know, it is Akaki, the son of the Sergueyevitch, the one who went off to make the revolution . . ."

"No, he didn't just go off, don't you remember how we selected him? He was the first who had harvested his potatoes. Well, we thought he should go, as the rest of us had too much work to be making the revolution."

"Yes, Mikhail cultivates his fields now," another adds.

"He's been on strike for a year, then? How did the revolution end up?" asks a third.

"They say they won?" yet another adds.

"Who do they say won?"

"You know, the usual people, the usual, who do you expect won?" shouts a voice from the crowd surrounding Akaki Sergueyevitch, who talks and talks as the circle gets bigger and bigger.

Oh, that was what he wanted, for the whole village to come to see him and listen to what he had to tell them, that the future began now, everything he had read in the Party newspapers.

"Now, my dear villagers, we don't need to sell our potatoes or corn!" Akaki shouts.

"So, Akaki, what will we do with our potatoes? We need to eat other things and need to buy clothes. What on earth! The things this Akaki says!"

"No, I'm sorry, from now on the state will take them."

"What, from now on the state will take our potatoes and corn? Fuck, we're going to have an easy time! And what will the state give us in return? Sorry, the *State*!"

"Well, you know, it will give you culture, it will give you culture."

"And won't we need to harvest any more corn or potatoes if they give us culture?"

"Yes, of course, you'll have to keep sowing and harvesting potatoes because the state will need potatoes."

"So we'll grow potatoes in exchange for culture. And what the hell use is culture to me, Akaki Sergueyevitch, if I still have to grow potatoes? Let the people who don't know us buy our crops! Culture! How stupid!" and the people kept questioning Akaki, as if they had to get their information from him on the new situation.

"So you say they will govern us from Moscow? But, Akaki, that's what the Tsar did. What's the difference?"

"And what about the train? When will the train reach here? I want to be a railway worker, my brother-in-law is one in Lunydeprokov, and he says it's a great life, that they live in the little station house and the passengers . . ."

But Akaki is no longer listening, he is tired and very hungry and doesn't understand why everyone is asking him questions, because he is only a rank-and-file soldier who had been chosen to make the revolution because he had been the first to harvest his potatoes. The village didn't want to be left out of what was happening in the city and sent him as their representative and, look, now he's back, and they don't even bother to invite him to supper. So Akaki leaves the crowd that has formed around him without anyone noticing and goes to see his parents. He left home a year ago and hasn't seen them since. They knew he was well from the letters he sent them, but that is about it.

Luckily, his parents are home and have cooked him the tastiest potatoes he has ever eaten. Akaki tells them about all the upheavals he has been part of, and his father says he needs him to start working soon, because the fields need another hand, Mikhail has done well, but family is always best. Akaki just wants to have a good nap to see whether he will wake up from this nightmare, it can't be true that nobody is aware that the world has changed and that he has contributed to the change. Oh, these people are so ignorant, luckily culture is on its way, and culture, you just wait . . . and Akaki falls asleep in the chair, his head on the table.

A couple of hours later, Akaki wakes up with a headache, but straight away he looks for a mirror so he can trim his beard, and a tub to wash in. When he is about to get dressed, he hesitates over whether to put on his revolutionary overcoat or wear the clothes he has always worn that his mother has just taken out of the trunk.

It's been so long, so long.

He has got thinner, the clothes that used to fit now billow around his bottom and back. Well, he'll soon put on weight and he won't ever be short of potatoes in Prokopov. And his boots and gaiters are so splattered with mud. Oh, he was looking forward to coming home so much.

While he is washing in the back of the cabin, he sees a girl walk by who looks as if she is pregnant and carrying a boy on her back and potatoes in her apron. She looks like . . . No, that can't be right.

"Natasha, are you Natasha?"

The girl's hair is untidy and her face is puffy. She doesn't reply and walks on through the mud.

"Yes, it's Natasha, Akaki, but don't speak to her, nobody speaks to her because Baron de Berezinov has made her a domestic servant and made her pregnant twice. Look she's become a right whore."

Akaki suddenly feels sick.

It can't be true: that bastard has got her pregnant twice, not because he raped her, but because she thought a peasant's daughter might become a baroness, his mother says, look what airs she gives herself, she keeps telling everyone the baron is going to marry her because he says he loves her, the wretched little fool, you see what a simpleton she is, Akaki, she thinks the baron really loves her and will take her and love her in his castle, ah, young people are so silly they think you can change the world in a flash and look what happened to her in a flash, Akaki. Yes, I know, you were very keen on her before, but, you know, things have changed, let others deal with their own blight, you know? You see, Akaki, she too thought she was making the revolution – in her belly.

Akaki has gone as red as a revolutionary flag, and like the country, doesn't know whether it's anger or shame, so he washes his face and neck hard with the water that splashes down from the roof and finishes getting dressed. He finds it hard to recognise himself, but the others in the village act as if he's not been away a single day, and instead of asking him what happened in St Petersburg or Minsk, or what the new government will do, they tell him not to bother with this year's harvest, because there are a lot of pests. Why is this all that interests them? Prokopov, you're part of this world and should know how it's faring . . . Oh, such backwardness, and no electricity, no light, such backwardness . . .

He thinks it is really incredible that he might be working in the fields this afternoon, as easily as that, after a whole year making the revolution, as if nothing at all had happened. He has the right to a free afternoon, come on, at the very least.

Akaki goes to the inn, a small shed with four chairs, and a flask of rough wine, one of firewater and another of vodka. There they will surely welcome him like a brave soldier. He's still got some of the allowance he was given to return home with, so he will invite them to drink vodka with him, maybe firewater, though he mustn't spend all he's got, and these peasants are so rude. No, he'll invite them for a glass of wine. They weren't even polite enough to ask him whether he'd had a good journey.

Inside the peasants are arguing fiercely – about the potato harvest, obviously, not about the revolution. Akaki shouts and says he is inviting everyone for a drop of wine. When the peasants hear that, they empty their glasses, take their chairs and sit around him.

They all look at him, expectantly, he's had a shave and now looks like a new man, the man who left the village to see the world.

"Akaki, tell us about the revolution," a couple of peasants ask.

"That's right, Akaki, do you think the revolution will raise the price of potatoes?" asks another.

"Don't be such a yokel . . . potatoes and more potatoes. Don't you see Akaki is tired after making the revolution, you don't ask a man that kind of question when he has just been making the revolution, don't be so thick," responds a third. "Come on, Akaki, tell us all about it."

And Akaki begins to tell them how he reached the city and fought against the troops who were there and mistreated people and how everyone came into the streets to greet them while the enemy got up to a thousand and one tricks to stop the revolution triumphing . . . Oh, and the Party, the Party, they are so kind and good and will give us culture so we can be free and we will have food from all over Russia because we will exchange goods, some will give us their produce, and this and that and we will give them potatoes in return so they give us clothes and culture, and electricity, the light that will brighten our lives, and a drop more wine please . . . Because together we must build a country to take us . . . working men, and the great Bolsheviks of the Future, and the theorists who write in the newspapers, and the workers who act like heroes, raising their tools against the mighty . . . And the peasants' eyes gradually filled with tears, from wine or emotion, what did it matter, and more people entered the inn to listen to him and drink his wine.

"We will work alongside all the upstanding men in the country and our efforts will commemorate the revolutionary fighters who have changed our great nation, efforts that will help us expand and expand and become the leaders of humanity and—"

"Yes, culture and electricity, plus potatoes, will make Prokopov a rich village."

"Hurrah, hurrah!"

Ah, Akaki thinks, the peasants have finally seen that the world has changed, the revolution has finally come to Prokopov, I am the seed that will germinate in the heart of the village, the seed fertilised by the culture that will rescue the village from its ignorance. Akaki is no longer the hungry soldier who came back this morning, but the centre of this assembly in the tavern in Prokopov.

Oh, how terrible I felt this morning when I arrived and saw that the square in Prokopov was exactly the same as when I left, oh, how terrible I felt when I saw Natasha, my Natasha, with the kid round her neck and potatoes in her apron, what a shock, what a nightmare, luckily the revolution has triumphed and the world has changed.

The wine stokes his courage and he stands on a chair and harangues the peasants from inside the inn: "I personally will start to organise a committee in Prokopov to see to the potato harvest and take the crop to a storehouse. I personally know men in the Party who will make Prokopov a prosperous, progressive village with culture everywhere. No longer will we have to pay tithes or income to the baron!"

Then silence descended on the inn. The peasants' eyes bulged out of their sockets. They thought, perhaps Akaki Sergueyevitch hasn't heard about the baron. No, he can't have, they think, or he wouldn't say that. Akaki, it's one thing to make the revolution and another to want to get rid of the nobility overnight . . . And, now, who'd have believed it, nobody can have told him about the baron, but nobody need tell Akaki Sergueyevitch what has happened here.

But nobody need tell him because it's almost time for him to see for himself. Otherwise he might never believe it. It's late and the sun is setting, and a horse can be heard trotting in the square. It's the baron, no longer wearing the clothes he wore that morning, but in uniform from head to toe, and where once he sported a coronet he now sports a red star. He can see him though the door, from the top of that chair, and his lackeys are with him and they too are in uniform and sport a red star and they are leading a cart which the peasants have stacked with sacks of potatoes and corn that they will take to the central organ of the Berezinov committee, to the baron's castle. The baron is a revolutionary now and not only is he the local Party leader but he is also responsible for collecting the taxes the Party has imposed. He owns the most beautiful horse in the district, say the peasants, and Natasha is walking behind the cart, a baby round her neck and a revolution in her belly, barefoot, the hem of her skirt covered in mud, pregnant again with the baron's child, the baron who is now Party head in Berezinov, and Akaki thinks about potatoes and culture as he jumps down from his chair and walks across the square, silent except for the sound of a horse trotting off towards the castle.

THE WAR AGAINST THE VOROMIANS

I.

Everything was well wrapped up, their suitcases packed and the lists of tools, notebooks, equipment and clothing complete. And food, bag after bag of biscuits and dried meat. The windows shut tight and the heating switched off. Everything cleared out, only two chairs and a mattress in the whole flat. She shared out her furniture among her neighbours, she doesn't know if she's coming back or what she'll find if she does.

She's been sitting in the dining room for a while, by the window. As soon as she sees the car coming she'll start to take the cases and bags downstairs. Over the last few days she's wondered thousands of times, what will happen? What's it all about this time? She's not received a letter from the professor for five years though she's been sending him two a month, perhaps she dispatched the last fifty or sixty – a running commentary – with the same lack of conviction with which she awaits a reply.

She is completely in the dark. The only information she has is that a car will come to pick her up at eight on the dot. But she hasn't a clue about who will replace her at the university or for how long she will be gone. Even so, at this stage, she doubts her final destination is Voromir. At any rate, all she can do is wait for the car. Out on the street some children are playing with a cloth ball, and the force of their kicks bears no relation to the speed at which the ball travels.

At last. As on other occasions, the car's rear windows are tinted. After shutting her flat and saying goodbye to the neighbours from the stairwell, she lets the driver heave the cases and packages into the boot. Inside, from the front seat, Inspector Niutonov welcomes her without a backward glance.

"You will fly, as you did the last time. They won't blindfold you, by now we have enough information to know it's common knowledge. Well, not exactly, I mean the foreign powers are in the know . . . but that's as good as to say that everyone knows."

"Ignat . . ."

"I know nothing, don't ask me. If you would like me to say that you will be returning home, I can, but I don't know for sure."

"Ignat, the professor . . . "

"The professor is well, his wife isn't. Problems with her circulation, heart failure, so remember, don't stop taking your medication until you're used to it again. And that's all I know, they are the two questions I expected to answer. One and a half. I still owe you a half I'll swap you for this sheet of paper. They won't interfere with your food or your clothes."

"Thank you, Ignat,"

They fall silent. Rosa watches the streets of Moscow fly by, the blocks of flats that disappear and turn into factories, factories that disappear into wasteland and, finally, wasteland that extends to the airport.

After passing through the controls, the car drives onto the landing strip. The guards stand to attention, recognise Ignat from afar. Stairs up to the plane, people waiting in the doorway as if they are expecting them, indeed, the car stops at the foot of the stairs.

"Door-to-door service. Good luck, Rosa. Regards to the professor."

Regards to the professor! The only plus side to all that is that she will see him again. And the worst part, obviously, is that she will see him again. The plane takes off. Almost three hours from the airport to the valley of Voromir, one and a half from the valley of Voromir to the entrance to the *oblast*. The airport that was built in the middle of the province had to be shut down, none of the purpose-built planes could control their flights, from the moment they flew over frontier rivers and valleys their dials went haywire.

The first time she went, she also travelled this way, but then the Voromir-Nov airport was simply a field. Now there's the military base and roads have replaced mud tracks.

She still remembers the professor and his wife sitting on the benches in the lorry.

"You will now notice something unusual," he told her the moment they crossed the river and the marshes flooded by the spring rains.

She will soon be experiencing that again, the same heaviness in her stomach and head, when the plane takes off and they are strapped in to their seats. It's like travelling by plane, he told her when she arrived in Voromir.

They have now got through the turbulence and the plane is flying above the clouds. She had the plane to herself. They had even allowed her to put her luggage on the seats next to her. She looks through the window, she can't but think that seen like that Russia is impossible, is a country that is far too large to do anything without inflicting lots of damage. The plain is never-ending.

It was a soft landing, no doubt about that. The myth exists that the pilots who fly to and from Voromir are the most experienced in the Union. Because the law doesn't recognise the anomaly affecting the area, the authorities always assign their best men there.

Rosa loads her luggage into the truck that will take them to Lenin-Voromir. Specially reinforced trucks able to endure despite the *anomaly*.

The second they enter Voromir and the truck drives through the valley and the marshes, over the bridge and the river, the anomaly will make its presence felt, and that's why Rosa is looking for the pills for blood circulation inside her bag and extracts her water flask. Two pills a day from now on until her body adapts to the change.

The professor's pills that thin out the blood. She and Professor Maxim manufactured these pills. Rosa used to feel queasier than the others and some peasants made her an infusion that became compulsory for anyone entering Voromir once they had confirmed that the symptoms disappeared and there were no side effects. A year later the professor had made similar pills with a formula that has by now been perfected. Moreover, they should take vitamin supplements: everything was much more effort in Voromir.

"Miss, everything is more effort in Voromir," said the peasant who lifted her head up so she could drink the infusion. "Everything is more effort in Voromir than in other parts of Russia. We are used to this because we've lived it from birth, but you're not from here, miss, you're not from here."

Those people had such a peculiar dialect! It was like nothing she had heard uttered before. She could understand there were different languages, but those people spoke with more open vowels. It wasn't much harder to understand the different lexis, and their declensions were similar to Russian, but the vowels, oh, the vowels, you never knew whether they wanted to say *keys* or *kiss*, and they were but two examples.

The road is full of checkpoints, though they don't search her until the vehicle reaches the bridge.

You won't find anything, what do they expect to ... "Just a formality." The soldiers on the bridge seemed almost apologetic.

And right, finally, as they drive out of the woods, the force of gravity in Voromir makes itself felt, suddenly the truck loses power, as if it has been loaded up with rocks, or the road, rather than being flat, has suddenly started up a gentle but constant incline. And the bag on top falls down and she puts it back and feels the difference. It weighs much more. Now they are well and truly in Voromir . . .

"The force of gravity is much greater in Voromir than in the rest of Russia, and much greater than in the rest of the world," the professor asserted after they stopped laughing. The professor was serious. He put a weight on the scale and lowered it with his hand until the hand reached the figure he was after. "Thirty per cent higher, gentlemen, I've just registered that. Twelve point seven. It's easy as dropping weights. We know for certain that it happens nowhere else on Soviet territory. We sent out explorers and have received letters from teachers, commissars, fieldworkers and researchers throughout the rest of the world. You now know the reason for those papers. No, it happens nowhere else, at sea or in any of the friendly nations or places we have come across, we have even collaborated with foreign universities on a long-term basis to see whether this is an oddity that is replicated in any other part of the globe . . . We have tested the antipodes of Voromir, for example. We have taken measures at different times of day and night, in case it was connected to the influence of the moon . . . It wasn't. Some parts of Voromir, very few, have a conversely lower level of gravitational pull than is normal, between seven point six and seven point eight instead of nine point eight. I must return next month." His eyes bulged out of their sockets.

"And, by the way, I've asked for an assistant. It's what one might call an onerous task, you know . . ."

Yes, it was onerous, really onerous. Particularly on the neck and back, as though you were carrying a heavy load on your head, every jolt on the road and your neck seemed about to snap. That's the first few weeks, blood pressure surges as well, then everything returns to normal.

However, that's not the worst of it, the worst thing is the voice change; vowels become more open. Day in, day out newcomers notice how it changes their accent and tone. They say it's the increased density of the air or the fact that the vocal chords are not used to the new force making them wilt, but the latter explanations have yet to be confirmed; the large number of doctors and physiologists transferred to the military base and Voromir are studying other matters deemed to be more important.

She finds the professor more quickly than she anticipated. She sees him as soon as the truck drives into Lenin-Voromir and they stop right by him. Hugs, kisses, and even tears. They don't mention Maria. In fact, she thought how the moment they stopped receiving letters, they also started to drop references to Maria in the letters they sent to him. The professor's voice had deepened and they found it hard to understand him.

"Oh, I'm so pleased to see you, especially with all the work that's piled up, there is so much, so much to be done here in Voromir."

"Professor . . ." she exclaims.

"Ah, I see no-one has informed you . . . That's typical of what it's like in Russia. So typical. You will be staying but don't worry, it won't be for very long. I reckon a year or so. I'll tell you all about it, but while we're here, I'll accompany you to your place". The truck drives ahead of them along the streets of the new district in Lenin-Voromir.

"So we're back," says Rosa. "I've been very downcast the last few years, hoping for a transfer."

"Everyone you met in Voromir has come back, you'll see, some stay, others leave: the designs of the Party are unfathomable. All of us who came on the first, second or third expedition have ended up living here. Here or on the military base. They say that by now the foreign powers know about it all, but even so they still don't want to make the discovery public. Now they're beginning to send rockets into space, it is very useful to have an area for testing like . . . Now we know it's unique in the world . . . Because we do know that for sure now." He looks at her to see how she reacts.

"Sure, as in one hundred per cent sure?"

"Yes, the whole area has been mapped and we have discovered how the gravitational pull varies from place to place. Many advances have been made in terms of the impact on the circulation of the blood and we've even developed medication so people don't speak with such open vowels. True, we don't take it because it's not yet compulsory, but within a year people will, and the Voromians will too. Obviously, they don't want to; nothing we can do about that . . . You stay on, Rosa. We've only a year to go. In a year's time the whole of Voromir will be like a desert, nobody is going to be allowed to stay."

Lenin-Voromir's streets are harder work than Moscow's. Fortunately, the truck has taken the luggage to the front door.

The house is one of a number built for the new engineers and teachers who have come to Lenin-Voromir. Those in the streets further up are for people working in the mines and on excavations the government has opened throughout the region. Theories abound about the presence of very heavy metal ores but, according to the professor, nothing has been proved. The anomaly remains a mystery. The professor bids them farewell till dinner and promises to come and give them a surprise.

Enough bags of coal have been left by the front door for them not to have to worry about the cold. The house is furnished, tastefully even. She still doesn't know what to expect, she has just seen the professor after five years and, as if it had been planned from the very start, she is back in Voromir – mattresses slightly on the tilt, reinforced furniture and backache. The professor's hunch is more pronounced than ever. Russians are the hunchbacks, as Voromians call them, because of the stoop that everyone born outside develops: their heads are too heavy and their shoulders give way. Voromians are stockier with thicker necks.

They knock at the door. Tasja gets up from the bed to open the door. Two Voromians with food, a duck and a heap of potatoes and turnips. Rosa gets up quickly and feels dizzy.

"No, miss, nothing to pay, Professor Albertinski ordered this and paid us. The professor told us he's expecting you for dinner, at his house, number ten, B Street, at around seven." Still, Rosa gives the local folk a few kopeks. When they are almost out of the door she invites them for a cup of tea.

"No, miss, we Voromians aren't allowed to sit down with you. You shouldn't ask us, it's frowned upon."

"Only for a cup of tea . . ."

"No, miss, thanks for the kopeks but sorry, we can't drink your tea . . ."

"Well, just wait," she says while she takes a tin from her suitcase and extracts a few tea leaves. "This is very good tea." She closes the door and bids them farewell. "Potatoes and turnips, better get used to them because I think we'll be eating nothing else for a long time."

She puts the duck and the root vegetables in the pantry and lays out her clothes. The water will soon heat up and then she can have a wash.

2.

By eight o'clock the street is deserted. The police are in their patrol cars and on street corners. Lenin-Voromir is an ugly town, the only area with any charm, where the original inhabitants live, is now hemmed in by new buildings with asphalt roads in contrast to the dirt tracks between the houses belonging to Voromians.

Lenin-Voromir wasn't like that the first time they came to work with the professor. It wasn't even called Lenin-Voromir, but Voralriu. It was the first town they saw in Voromir, with men, women and children of Voromir who had lived their whole lives under the influence of a force of gravity that was greater than in the rest of the world.

They conducted surveys with all those people, people astonished by the newcomers' curiosity.

"Have you noticed anything strange when you walk or when you jump?"

"No, lady, I walk and jump like everyone else. I've never noticed anything strange."

"Do you often feel tired?"

"When I'm cutting grass I do, because cutting grass wears you out."

"Have you ever wanted to leave Voromir?"

"No, lady, I am from Voromir, I don't know where I would go. Now that you have come, Voromir has changed and perhaps we should go into the mountains, because there's not enough water in Voralriu. But apart from that, lady, I have never thought of leaving."

There *was* nothing strange about those people. The students who carried out the surveys and even Professor Albertinski who directed them had to keep changing part of their explanation of the *anomaly*. That's what it had to be called; it was forbidden to use words like "difference" or "specificity". Gravity in Voromir was an anomaly. What's more, one could even start to conclude that the anomaly only existed because people had experienced it from childhood but hadn't realised that it was the case. It was often said that if the region had been desert, it would have been a source of pride for the Soviet people to possess land with such unusual characteristics. Even land inhabited by those people, that is, if the dialect they spoke had not developed into such an incomprehensible blather. And, besides, the Voromians were such a contrast to all the peoples in the border territories, who were very familiar and used dialects that were all very similar and like Russian, with which they had no difficulty.

In Voromir everything was much more complicated, what with those damned vowels that were far too open. And there was something that was even more difficult to grasp: according to all the comparative analyses they had conducted on the Voromians and the neighbouring peoples, all the parameters gave Voromians a slight, though solid advantage. It was as if that people had become accustomed to the extra effort demanded by the land they inhabited. Strange, but true. Moreover, it was unusual to find Voromians working in neighbouring provinces. On the contrary, it was peasants from the surrounding areas that migrated in search of work in Voromir.

"And when you came, did you notice that it was very different?" Rosa would ask the peasants who had come to the province in their youth.

"Yes, lady, everything was much more effort, took more time, was more exhausting . . . We had headaches and backache, but they went after a year or two. It's a struggle to become a Voromian – first, your legs must get stronger . . ."

"And you must speak differently."

"Yes, lady, we didn't understand them to begin with and nobody knew why they spoke that way, but, lady, now I understand, and people from outside don't understand me. They say it's a real effort to think like a Voromian and that's why they end up speaking differently, but don't take any notice of me, lady, I'm only a peasant and don't know a thing about all this stuff."

One survey followed another, the same questionnaire had to be given to all the fifteen thousand inhabitants who lived in the area including one question about when they'd come there. The most peculiar part, what astonished the professor and Rosa and Tasja, was the way Voromians spoke about the world outside. Not one wanted to leave Voromir, though they all knew the disadvantages of living in a land like it. If you were born in Voromir you were condemned to lift heavier weights than anyone in the rest of the world. She still laughs when she remembers a peasant who told the professor what it was like to live there and why they didn't go to Molar or Severnor, cities in the neighbouring *oblasts*. The professor was weary:

> "I'm asking if you notice anything different. Look, if I lift this object it is more of an effort for me than it is for you," he said, taking one of the many objects on the table. In those early days, the physicists' and geographers' labs shared a large barracks the military had just built. "Can you see that if I put this item on the scales it shows one point three kilos and in Moscow, Vladivostok or Sebastopol, it shows only one. I'm asking you to explain the reason for those extra three hundred grammes ..." The professor was livid – one of the biggest discoveries of the twentieth century, and people couldn't care less.
>
> "Excuse me, you must have travelled outside Voromir, you must have been to the provinces of Molar or Severnor to sell grain or skins."
>
> "No, sir, I haven't, but I know some people who have and

they say Molar is very pretty too, though Severnor is less so and . . ."

"Please, do continue . . . And this friend of yours?"

"Ivan Mostrovitch."

"Yes, of course. Did this Ivan Mostrovitch notice any substantial difference between the weight he transported and the weight he sold . . . ?"

"I don't understand you."

"Whether the same grain weighs more here than it does there . . ."

"That's right, but he never went to school, Your Excellency."

"But you don't need to go to school: a sack weighs more and then it weighs less." Everybody was staring at them, physicists and geologists put their samples and graphs down and laughed at the professor's insistence.

"Excellency, Ivan always transports the same sack."

"Hey, do you see this?" he asked as he put the weight on the scale. "Here, this is one point three kilos. Do you see?" he asked him as he lifted the scale slightly. "Outside Voromir it is only one kilo."

Then the peasant got up and went to the weighing machine and put a one-kilo weight on each side and looked at the professor.

"Here, a weight weighs what a weight has to weigh, Excel-lency," he said as he pointed at the perfect balance between the two sides of the weighing machine.

The applause frightened the peasant, and it was then that they discovered that Voromians had no tradition of applauding and only clapped to beat woodcocks and deer out of the woods. The fact that everyone laughed at what he said calmed him down and Professor Albertinski didn't ask any more questions.

He looked at Rosa and shut his notebooks.

"There is no anomaly."

"No, Professor, there isn't."

"No, everything weighs more here, including the responses."

He joked as he put away that day's questionnaires and collected the papers. It was 1932. Spring 1932. All there was in Lenin-Voromir was the barracks and the houses along the river. Today, the houses in the new neighbourhoods tower above those houses, as if the force of gravity had pulled the older building's foundations further down. Workers on higher ground have even asked for their homes to be demolished and for new ones to be built on the flat, so they don't have to walk uphill so much. Indeed, they are now uninhabited, except for three old couples and the odd straggler.

In 1933, after they had seen that the geographers and historians were making no progress, they decided that, for the sake of safety, it was better for all Voromians to go and live in Stalin-Voromir. Everybody should go and live in Stalin-Voromir, the inhabitants of the smallest villages, the families who lived in the middle of the woods and even those who had built their huts by the side of the river. It was for their own good; they were told that the anomaly might damage their health. Even though Voromians had lived in the province from time immemorial and had never been more or less ill than people in the rest of the Empire, the possibility was now broached that it might be some kind of problem. The anomaly might create problems.

No-one believed it, but no-one dared say anything. The purges obeyed mechanisms that were more unfathomable than the anomaly, and there were purges in the army, the administration, the university, and even in Voromir. The few Voromians who had dared to protest were invited "to come to Moscow and explain their demands and proposals in more detail". Another of their euphemisms.

Professor Albertinski himself had been purged. Rather than let him return to Moscow, he was confined to Voromir so he could continue to study the anomaly as long as he wanted. The professor and his colleagues had been allowed to teach. They had always understood that to mean they weren't thought to be a real danger, as they knew only too well that the professor's life could depend on what they did. They became accustomed to living like that, exhausting every possible interpretation of what the administration or Party said or did. Finally, it was Rosa's turn. At least they had granted her a house.

A house, and that was no small concession. The first to be sent there didn't have houses. They lived and slept in the barracks with the military. Rosa, who spent long stretches there and then returned to Moscow, had lived in a house belonging to Voromians, to Olga and Narod. They had a young daughter, Zoya, for whom Olga and Rosa acted as mothers. Rosa couldn't have children, she didn't want to have children, she had seen what could happen to them, carted here or there and never seen again. They lived in one of the prettiest spots near Stalin-Voromir, also an area with one of the highest levels of gravitational pull – more than thirteen point one, approaching thirteen point two. Olga was forever preparing infusions, and water was always on the boil.

The second time they returned, during the war, Olga and Narod had disappeared. The two families now living in the house had been driven out of the woods. The professor said Olga and Narod had been taken to the farms of Kazakhstan, which is where they were gradually taking

THE WAR AGAINST THE VOROMIANS

all Voromians. As they suspected, the authorities were using the census and documentation that they themselves had put together. In fact, the majority of the people in Voromir were Russians and Ukrainians who could be grateful they weren't in Moscow or, worse still, at the front.

The repopulation of Voromir with Russian speakers had begun. They changed the names of towns and villages. Roads were asphalted as quickly as the wartime lack of supplies would allow, and Voromians were sent off to front-line units like so much cannon fodder. No-one could carry as much weight as they could; when everyone else was dead tired, a Voromian always came to the rescue. The medical experiments and surveys had ended. Voromians were expendable, they had had the luck or misfortune to come up against the anomaly and that was all there was to it.

Before she enters the square where A, B and C streets start, a patrol accosts her, asks for her papers and where she is going at that time of night. They are Voromians, Voromian police who have slightly lost their accent.

"No, they're not Voromians, they are Russians, like me and you. Russians who are losing their Russian accents," says the professor when Rosa tells him. "I sometimes feel all of us here are turning into Voromians."

"The things you say, Professor."

"No, I mean it. There are hardly any Voromians left. Two or three hundred. Whether the population here is Russian or Voromian I couldn't say. But Russian in origin. Almost all are deportees. Like me. Like you, Rosa. You must have already been thinking much the same, when they came for you this morning." The professor's hallway is full of food. It's built like the pantries they used to build in Voromian houses.

"Three hundred? Only three hundred?"

"I said two or three hundred. More likely two. They are difficult to count because they live in the woods and are always moving around. For the moment, the commissars haven't found any pretext for going after them, but any day now the order will come from Moscow and that will be the end of that."

"But, Professor . . ."

"Yes, Rosa, I know. I know what you're going to say. If you want, we can discuss it and I will explain, but don't blame me, because I have had to bite my tongue repeatedly since I came here."

"Professor . . ."

"Yes, Rosa, I know. I couldn't write to you, obviously, you know what the post is like. But lots of things happened here after the end of the war. You already saw how it was going at the time."

"Professor, there were those relocations during the war. When I left more than fourteen thousand Voromians were living here. The surveys I worked on all that time . . ."

"Lies."

"But, Professor . . ."

"Lies, I tell you. The thousand missing at the front, O.K. But as soon as the war was over, Voromir was declared a priority interest zone. The anomaly was of decisive importance for the space race. They scattered Voromians across Russia. If you think that was wrong, remember that at least they didn't kill them or transport them to labour camps. We know they are on collective farms and that's about as much as we know, right – vodka and gherkins for everyone."

The professor's maid lays the table and prepares bread and cabbage; it's the woman who brought us food earlier on. Rosa could almost say she looks like Maria, she'd already thought that and said as much with her glance. But she isn't Maria.

"So how do you know?"

"In the same way that you know that Maria is dead. Yes, don't look at me like that. I received all your letters, all opened by the authorities – that goes without saying – but I received every single one. No, you don't need to tell me that you didn't receive mine, Professor Tomski is of the opinion that the anomaly is to blame, letters from outside feel the extra pull and those that want to leave can't."

"Is he here as well?"

"Everybody is here. And now even you are. Few remain outside, of those who've been coming here. Professor Tomski's theory is that we all end up returning because the gravitational pull is stronger. We'll go to his house tomorrow. But today we will have dinner here. Besides, I have a surprise for you, a surprise that's arriving now," he says as he looks through the window.

The door bangs downstairs and someone climbs the stairs. A svelte, pretty young girl appears through the curtains. She kisses the professor and immediately turns towards Rosa. She stands and looks at her as if she is expecting her to say something.

Something, but she can't think what. Something. Yes, she is waiting.

"Zoya!" shouts Rosa. "God, it's Zoya!"

And that was that, tears, kisses and hugs and Zoya and more Zoya and memories: "Do you want some more water? Do you want some more water?" Zoya laughs, remembering what she always used to ask when she offered people an infusion.

"No, I'm feeling queasy, blasted gravity."

"And I would run out of the cabin, laughing 'Blasted gravity, blasted gravity', but believe me I didn't know what you were saying, and Mother always chased after me to slap me on the bottom."

"That was years ago, Zoya. You're so pretty. And you've grown so."

Tasja also gives her a hug. The professor grins broadly at them both and waves his hands in pure glee.

"Who'd have thought it?" the professor exclaims, "Hey, who'd have thought it?"

"And how are your parents, Zoya? Are they well?"

"Yes, Rosa, they are, they are on the collective farm and full of nostalgia because the woods there aren't like the woods here, and they have to work on a farm. They're both looking after cows."

"What about you? Why have you come back?"

"The professor knew I was studying at university and he asked for me. I came two years ago, two years, seven months, to be exact."

"She's a qualified geologist, the top mark for her year, you can't say she didn't carry geology in her blood. All Voromians should be geologists, right?"

"Ohhh, Professor."

"That's right, and not many are as bright as she is. She says she wants to marry a Russian, but we'll sort that out. To marry a Russian when there are still Voromians around seems rather . . ." he says with a laugh. "But let's have dinner, let's have dinner. Maria has laid the table." He raises his glass of vodka, "Na zdarovie!"

They all shout "Na zdarovie!" and sit down.

They eat heartily; no-one says a word because they are all considering how far they can go in what they can say. The professor is sitting between Zoya and Rosa.

The professor feels ill at ease as host. He is thinking about Rosa and the changes. He watches Rosa put another pill in her glass. Changes are always too sudden. Once there was a time when he thought of constructing family genealogies, to see whether the people who withstood the anomaly best had forebears from Voromir, but that was a nigh-on impossible project. They tried to discover how many Russians and inhabitants of neighbouring provinces had come in recent decades, but the political commissars told them it would be better to avoid that angle and he did. It was as clear as daylight with Zoya, apart from her usually living in Voromir, simply the force of gravity, that alone . . . She had adapted well to the farm but within a fortnight of returning was fine in Voromir. He has said nothing and nor has she: the best adaptation to Voromir since they started carrying out tests and surveys. That is why they replied to her and let her come back, you can bet the latest analyses completed in Voromir are Zoya's. Conversely, Rosa requires endless periods before she adapts.

"Nobody would think you have been away so long, you speak like a Voromian."

"I am a Voromian, Rosa. I am one hundred per cent Voromian."

"Even though our Zoya now wants to marry a Russian officer."

"Don't take any notice of the professor, that's just local gossip. I'll be after Sergei as soon as I can. I will wait. The Russian officer can go to hell as far as I'm concerned. He hangs around me all day, like a lap dog. Besides, he does nothing but curse Voromir; why the fuck did they send him here, this place is for peasants, constantly complaining that he's dying to get back to Vilnius. To Vilnius! I ask you!"

"How are your parents?"

"They are fine. Father says the world is lighter outside Voromir. My mother is happy enough. He's sometimes nostalgic, especially about the food. He complains that everything is better in Voromir. The cheese is stronger and the vodka tastier. I'm not surprised: we breakfast, lunch and dine on Voromir. I ought to have said: they are fine now. When they were thrown out of their home and transported there, they thought they would die. They weren't alone in that, everyone did. At least those they deported to Kazakhstan. People laughed at them because of their vowels . . . They dispersed them around the same region, a handful in each village . . . Two families in one, three in another . . . And that way you knew there were a dozen Voromians in the neighbouring village and they told you they knew for sure there were twenty plus further on . . ."

"Tell me about it."

"You haven't heard?"

"What was there to hear?"

"It's difficult to explain. It's difficult because it is so sad and because I prefer not to think about it, but since we've had to accept it whether we like it or not . . . They have finally found a way to make Voromir Russian. Completely. Obviously, the only way is to empty it out. Hadn't you understood that?"

"I've not really had much time to think about it."

"Well, now you'll have all the time in the world. This is definitive, for real. We Voromians will all be removed elsewhere and Russians will take our place for a year. Until they throw you out too."

"I don't understand, Zoya, I really don't understand . . ."

They want the region to be completely abandoned and all the people in the neighbouring *oblasts* to be Russian. Russian speakers, and not only from White Russia or the Ukraine, they want them to come from the provinces of Novgorod or Riazanov."

"I still don't understand."

"The only Voromians they might leave here, though this remains to be seen, because even they may not be left, are childless couples, single men and widowers and the elderly. The last Voromians who will gradually die out."

"A homeopathic dilution."

"The most diluted possible. In fact, they want the last inhabitants of Voromir to be Russian and for the population in the bordering provinces to be entirely Russian as well."

3.

A lorry has come to a halt in the street. Its driver then has to manoeuvre strenuously to get out of the mud ruts that have formed under its wheels. The shouts of the soldiers pushing and spreading branches in front of the lorry and the roars from the vehicle wake Rosa up.

From her window she can see them talking to each other and she only has to lift her head to watch the whole scene. They are talking, shouting and laughing at the lorry as it zigzags and slips and slides all over the road. They have been living there for some time; their accents are beginning to sound Voromian.

She must be alone at home and it must be past ten o'clock. One of the soldiers slips and almost falls down; he's had to catch hold of the other who almost falls too. The cigarette being smoked by the one helping drops in the mud. They are both laughing, splitting their sides.

This story has a foretold conclusion, she thinks. The designs of the government will be carried out in a disciplined way, what is decided is decided, but she can't help but think how pointless the whole thing is. Because although it is true that the government will order these laughing soldiers to throw out all the Voromians, how will it order the force of gravity in Voromir not to pull them back?

An old story told about a boy and girl from Voromir suddenly pops into her head. It's a legend, a legend that is going nowhere, Romeo and Juliet in Voromir, parents who don't want them to marry, that same story told time and again around the world. But why was the story of Var and Mirtila so important to the people of Voromir?

One of the soldiers looks around as if he were expecting someone, but he isn't, he just heads into the bushes for a piss. Rosa can see him from behind, how he zips up and how the other soldier offers him another cigarette.

The families of Var and Mirtila, the researchers told them, had lived from yesteryear on one of the plains created by the rivers in the valleys of Voromir. As far as Mirtila's father was concerned, Var was the most insignificant of her suitors. And Mirtila was the least favoured wife-to-be of all the candidates in the eyes of Var's parents. She was invisible.

Nevertheless, the love the young people felt for each other led them to scurry every night betwixt birch and fir, pool and footbridge, to a meeting-place where they made love. The attraction was magnetic, absolute. Over time, Var and Mirtila turned into two rocks in the valley where they are said to have lived – nothing that hasn't been recounted a thousand times throughout Russia. But didn't it have another meaning here?

Despite everything, Voromians aspired to return home, a kind of diaspora in reverse that the government couldn't block. And the Russians sent there went reluctantly.

One of the soldiers slipped and went head over heels in the mud. Rosa hears the key in the door. It must be Zoya.

There is always a morning mist in Voromir. The first mornings here, your head is also full of mist and feels as if it is about to burst, and now Rosa put the mattress on a steeper incline. They say it is the gravity that attracts the mist, but geographers and physicists can't agree. She needs hot water. And breakfast. She is tired; her arms feel like lead as do her legs, clothes, everything. Even the water from the shower hurts her skin. She should have known not to turn it on so hard.

Then, of course, the sun disperses the mist and Voromir is beautiful. As lovely as any of the neighbouring *oblasts*.

The professor is with Zoya waiting for her, she should get a move on, she knows how he likes to grumble. He says they must go up into the mountains so he can tell them about their final assignment. It must be a census, as there's nothing else she can do here.

The engine grunts and splutters. She can still remember the time when an army lorry gave up on these same steep roads and slid back down. They almost went over the precipice.

"Have you taken your pills?"

"Three at a time, Zoya."

The professor looks at her and strokes her hair. She must look dreadful for the professor to cosset her so. Yes, she is feeling sick because of all the potholes and bends in the road, it feels like her brain is about to seep out of her ears, and her legs are swollen, her varicose veins are killing her and that's why she put on thin trousers even though it is bitterly cold.

The wooden huts on the mountain sides have been demolished or replaced by ugly, breeze-block houses. New roads reach up to the peaks and ridges, earth that curls down the slopes like blood from a face just nicked by a razor blade. The questions are the usual, name, age, children, parents, cousins, illnesses, etc.

Voromians are pleasant, the odd one even looks at her as if he recognises her. One couple are called Var and Mirtila, like so many. They ask her where they will be taken. She can't think what to reply . . .

THEATRE OF SHADOWS

For Gloria F. Famadosiva

She is in the photograph with my mother and me. Her name is Svetlana Privalova. Mrs Privalova was a photographer and had just arrived in Korassevo from Orel. In the photograph we are in the tavern kitchen. My mother is giving her a spoonful of onion soup that she has cooked for supper and I am laughing because Mrs Privalova burns her tongue. There are photos of the village, the surrounding area, the people who lived here, some are dead and the rest of us have grown old.

One Monday we had seen two lorries driving up along the road from the north. The noise got louder and louder, then it went silent in front of the tavern. Seven people alighted with their suitcases and said they wanted to rent every room. Mother organised it and had to send other guests to sleep in my uncle's house. Who could refuse rooms to people bringing orders from Moscow?

Nobody. Consequently, everyone joined in, delighted, pleased, indifferent, under compulsion or reluctantly. Mrs Privalova was travelling throughout Russia, in that year of 1932, to film and photograph the revolution, all those years after the event. They had to fill the gaps, the revolution didn't carry a camera and they had to find the landscapes, scenarios, villages and men who could represent the great deed. She spoke as if delivering a speech she had read a lot before inflicting it on Korassevo – from sheets of paper that were worn from so much shuffling.

I can't say they treated us well, my mother was desperate, they were asking the tavern to provide what the best hotel in Orel could never have given them. They weren't interested in me at all; I've got very big ears and a big forehead. I'm not saying this out of spite; they really didn't treat us at all well . . . Mrs Privalova insulted me and called me Big Ears; not that I was the only one – she called others Hunchback, Fatty and Smelly.

And that was why they summoned every villager and half disguised us and forced us to run around like lunatics as they filmed from every possible angle. One of the lorries carried all kinds of uniforms, rifles that had been rendered unusable, flags and other gear to characterise villagers as goodies or baddies, soldiers or officers, dead or wounded. One moment they had us defending a house, the next attacking ruins on the outskirts of Korassevo, the next walking along a path that enters the village from the north, and finally looking in wonder at the hammer and sickle.

Mother and I made up their rooms, but they asked us not to touch or look at anything. We didn't touch a thing, though it was impossible to do their rooms without looking at the photos, even if it was only out of the corners of our eyes. The people from the village were there in every imaginable pose. Some seemed good, others very wicked; some disguised as the wealthy were poor as church-mice; others, irreconcilable enemies, toasted the revolution together like good Bolsheviks. The truth is that the photos were lovely. I'm no expert, but my mother and I liked them a lot. Never before had that number of photos been taken in Korassevo. The whole village had been transformed into a huge theatre that, when Mrs Privalova and her crew left, sunk back into its usual peace and quiet.

We shouldn't worry about how the photos would be used. They were only for the archives, they told us, but the fact is many of those images were published in books, magazines, newspapers, encyclopaedias and television programmes here and abroad. I suppose that other photos taken in other cities and villages must have met the same fate. What could that old man say who, according to the captions, was a counter-revolutionary bourgeois? And the fellow they said was a doctor but who didn't even know how to read or write? And the faces of the dead in the foreground, people who were still running around the village. Everybody's silence regarding that period was one of those unwritten agreements kept for years and years in small villages.

They came one Monday and took the road north the following Saturday and the village was left as full or as empty as usual, depending on how you saw it. I found the photographs and had to raise Cain to prevent mother from giving them back, or worse, from burning them. They must have fallen behind a drawer, and, as they took thousands, I suppose they never missed them.

There were thirty-two photos all told, one of which matched the newspaper cutting a frequent guest brought to our tavern fifteen years after all that upheaval. We heard no more of Mrs Privalova, that is, until today, when she *was* the one in the photo, a close-up. She looks in a bad state. It is a police photo and they have accused her of falsifying photographs of the revolution!

Whatever the reason behind it, the faces of people from Korassevo have appeared in many publications; there is one – the one of the peasants exchanging their hoes for rifles – that was exhibited next to Stalin's face!

But the one I prefer is another that this frequent visitor brought us. It is a photo of the kitchen but it is a trick photo. I'd already seen some of them because the crew hung a few on the tavern walls. Mrs Privalova has been replaced by a grateful soldier and the whole scene, according to the caption, is about how a family that helped the Bolsheviks during the revolution also helped the troops during the war against the Germans.

You know, photographers from Moscow have been back; evidently, they now want to follow the progress of a village that was decisive in the revolutionary struggle and against the Nazis. They are a bit more polite, but they don't want me in any of their photos either; you know, our ears continue to grow as the years roll by . . .

JOSSEF BERGCHENKO

Jossef Abrahmovitch Bergchenko (Ternopil, 1891 – Stalingrad, 1942) was the first son of one of the best-known Jewish families in Ternopil at the turn of the century. Bergchenko wrote stories for children's magazines and also texts for schoolbooks for his own native Ukraine. His name is renowned because it was the name given for years to a manual that he thought up about ways to learn to read. The "Bergchenko" was one of the most reprinted books in Russia.

The narratives that Bergchenko wrote for adult readers never achieved critical acclaim, because the critics only saw them as a reworking of themes from his children's stories. We know that that wasn't the case, that he was a precocious reader of Kafka, that his studies of Gogol, Pushkin and Ismalov are still relevant and that Isaak Babel appreciated his writing and the deeply religious, almost mystical, feeling in his stories. Of the stories we have included, the first, "The Riders", "The Track in the Middle of the Forest", "The Twins" and "The Resurrection of Souls" belong to the collection *Popular Stories* (1922). "Sergei Aleksandr's Last Supper" (1937), a free version of *The Fiesta in the Time of the Plague*, was commissioned by the city of Ternopil to celebrate the centenary of the death of its author, Aleksandr Pushkin. Between this story and the previous ones Bergchenko published *Stories of Animals That Don't Want to be Pets* (1926) and *Traditional Stories* (1929).

Bergchenko died during the siege of Stalingrad at the school where he taught and that today, now rebuilt, still bears his name.

THE RIDERS

"Why do the riders gallop so fast?" asks the merchant.

"Because the Tsar has issued an *ukase* to all horsemen. He wants the swiftest, bravest riders on their best steeds now. He wants them to go to war on his behalf, merchant," replies a little girl who wants to exchange salt for dry cheese.

Everyone is outside their huts: men and women dressed for the festive occasion. They greet the riders galloping down from the crags to the village with shouts of glee and encouragement. The oldest leave their huts as soon as they hear the din made by the horses, pull up blades of grass and throw them in the air as a blessing and shout like the young women as the horsemen ululate, spurring on their mounts that seem to bolt, slaver and sweat clouds of dust and earth, the strongest horses in the world, summoned by the Tsar. The riders stand in their stirrups and wave their hats whenever they ride by the crowds, summon their companions, their wives, their future wives.

The riders' mothers and young women go to the salt stall and put double handfuls in the bundles they have prepared for their sons, unleavened bread, dry cheese and, now, salt. The horsemen ride level with the merchant's stall, and without dismounting or halting their gallop, take the bundles their mothers and betrothed are offering them and ride on, but no longer in circles around the settlement, nor along the road that leads to the city, but into the distance, into the hills at the end of the steppes, where the sky blends into the earth.

"But where are the horsemen riding?" the merchant asks.

And it isn't the little girl who replies but the riders' mothers and young women: "They are off into the mountains, merchant, where the soldiers will never find them, the Tsar only wants them for his war. They won't be allowed to ride free and in peace, there they will make them ride to war, his captive warriors."

And the whole band of horses and riders seems like a single animal surging on as fast as it can. Their hooves throw up grass and damp earth and the ground seems to shake under the feet of the villagers. The riders arch their bodies, couple down close together until their faces are next to their steeds' and share the air they breathe and the movements they make to gallop faster, the riders feel the caress of manes and the horses the faces of their riders, and all want to flee, to cross the steppe of level grass like a cushion that makes the centaurs' gallop even swifter, and the whole band binds more tightly together, comes so close it is like one compact mass in flight that finally melds into the steppe.

THE TRACK IN THE MIDDLE OF THE FOREST

The most ferocious bears live deep in the heart of the taiga.

Not a single one has ever been hunted.

Hunters know they are very dangerous, they say the bears think, like men, and that is why they never go near them, in the heart of the taiga. They are frightened, are aware of the dangers of paths that never end, of tracks that fork time and again until the man who dares penetrate so far finds himself turning in circles, sometimes in spirals, until the time comes when he dares not move until a rescue party reaches him. That is the taiga; no-one wants to risk going in, the only way to enter the taiga is by cutting, burning and destroying it. Even so, the taiga wins out.

They say that those who get lost in the taiga pray and believe their prayers will save them, but not so. God is great, but the taiga is even greater, and they can pray as fervently as they curse, howl and rage, the taiga is deaf to their words, and that is why hunters can't ever agree to go in too deep, they hesitate, argue, curse, but always retreat to the outer fringe of trees. The most ferocious bears are deep inside, men who changed into bears, and that is why they are so vicious, because they are evil like men and think like men, their instinct is not an animal's, is not what an animal is born with, but a mixture of the viciousness of men and the cruelty of animals, they are wild beasts but it is said that when they look at you, it is as if they are thinking hard, and their eyes are glinting.

Once, before they had built the villages that surround the taiga, many, many years ago, there was a party of beaters that went into the taiga to hunt for skins. Everybody knew that what they really wanted were the skins of the bears who live in the centre of the forest, legends abounded about the thickness and value of these skins. They say they began walking in the first days of spring, because they thought that it might take them a few weeks to find the lairs of those bears, if not months. They preferred to crunch snow than be left high and dry when autumn came.

They trekked for days and days. They say the hunters watched their supplies run out, and that day after day, for far too long, they only ate birds they could catch and the mushrooms that grew all around. Weeks went by and the hunters continued to trek further into the forest, penetrating deeper and deeper inside. Their beards were long and their hair matted. They hadn't washed for days and their clothes were filthy from sleeping in the open, from walking through mud and thickets, from the blood of the animals they had killed in order to eat. They stank of forest, of dry leaves and flattened plants, of sweat and of the smoke from the fires they lit each night to keep warm. And they went even further into the taiga, even on days when the mist hid the sun, further in, even though they were lost, and didn't know where they were going. And they kept losing items of clothing and had to wrap up in non-cured skins of animals they were killing with knives, spears and bows, because their powder had got wet and they had thrown their guns away, along with the lead ammunition that had weighed too much . . .

And finally, to communicate with each other, and because they were afraid of the bears, which couldn't be far away, they mimicked the screeches of owls and the hisses of wild cats, and almost stopped speaking. They decided to light no more fires so the animals couldn't detect their presence and they ate raw meat.

By the time they finally saw the bears, they were crawling on all fours, wore the skins of other animals, had turned wild, stank and were filthy. The bears sniffed and encircled them but did them no harm: there was no difference between them. The hunters didn't recognise each other and thought the bears were other hunters and the hunters were bears.

But that is only a fable, because nobody ever emerged from the taiga to say what really happened. That is why men are afraid to enter the taiga, because within every forest there is a track that will lead them inside, into its heart.

THE RESURRECTION OF SOULS

The landscape could not be more desolate. Beyond the marshes, the rivers and other huge estates that seemed to distance you further from that emptiness, one had the feeling that there was nothing anywhere, a scrap of land in the back of beyond, with remnants of forests and culti-vated land, oppressive in summer and foggy in winter: the repetition of the same image to be found in so many other parts of the country, the repetition of days that go by when you think there is no possibility of change.

Serfs brought their poverty to that sadness. A procession of dirty, smelly, starving men, women, children and elderly walking towards the fields as soon as the sun began to rise. Every morning they would leave their *izbas* and trudge along the front of the porches of the master's mansion until the overseer arrived. Then, the perennial tasks, the toil that lasted a lifetime, digging, sowing, harvesting, taking the animals to graze, to be milked . . . Whatever, every year from time immemorial, nobody remembered when their great-grandfathers or perhaps their great-grandfathers settled there. The children that didn't die before reaching manhood grew healthily, and the toils every day, every season, every year strengthened them, and then wasted and aged them until they were small once again and could fit into an even smaller pit, the land to which they had a right, that they had bought. In fact, the memory never changed; men and women who grew old working their master's land until they earned the right to be buried right there, on the other side of a hill, in a simple ceremony, that scrap of soil was all they could ever come to own.

It had been like that forever, and there was no sign in any of the elements that made up that dismal panorama that they might ever change. Three men cost less than a mule, a woman little more than a dog, the health of a pig was immeasurably more valuable than that of the children wallowing in the mud next to the *izbas*. Only life had any value, the vital impulse of those souls who had to spend their time, from childhood to old age, extracting profit from the master's land for the master, that was the only end they could aspire to. When they had exhausted all their strength digging, transporting, reaping, pounding or threshing, when the men were old and could work no more, when the women were barren and so worn out they could barely even launder clothes, all they wanted to do was to die quickly, to end their lives for once and for all so as not to be a burden to their children, so as not to take from the mouths of their grandchildren the scant food the master distributed every Sunday that kept them alive, the weekly ration of bread, salt and meat.

The life of the serfs was pitiful, like the landscape, four days of holiday a year, to celebrate winter and summer, sowing and reaping, and that was that, nothing else. The only time to rest and relax was at night, by the fireside, when they had eaten dinner and they huddled together to keep warm. The oldest women told stories and fables, the stories they had heard when they were young, when they sat between their grandmas and grandads so as not be cold. Everyone fell asleep while the voice, like a litany, revisited every detail and possible variation of plot and conclusion, nothing that was ever novel, the young girl who marries the prince, the child who defeats the giant, the same old stories, the stories that try to give a glimmer of hope to the most unfortunate.

From time to time, though nobody knew why, someone would

retell the legend of the man in the calash, the man who travelled throughout Russia, the Urals and Siberia, the whole of the Ukraine, White Russia and Georgia, from China to the Urals and from the Urals to the Carpathians, the man who went as far as the land of the Cossacks and Tartars, of the Hungarians and Turks, to free the souls of the serfs. The legend, that the serfs came to believe as if it were a rock-hard truth, told how the man in the calash, the Saviour, had been the serf of a landowner who owned huge amounts of land. The owner was a merciless master who starved his serfs, who set dogs on little children, who killed women and children the moment there were too many people on his estate and he couldn't sell them. If there was nobody to give birth, there would be no newly born. When he was young, the Saviour, the man in the calash, took his revenge on the landowner, killed all his children, threw them down a well one by one and then threw rocks after them so they wouldn't be found until he was far, far away. He fled abroad where he made a fortune, an incalculable fortune to rival those that the Tsar or that any European emperor might have hoarded. The legend concluded by recounting how the man in the calash, the Saviour, as he was the child of an *izba* and the men from the *izbas* had generous hearts, longed to make amends for his crimes. He had killed the landowners' children and wanted to pay for those deaths by recovering the lives of others and that was why he travelled throughout Russia, from the Dniester to Siberia, to free the serfs who toiled day after day across that desolate landscape. The man in the calash bought serfs from their masters, he offered them such large amounts of money that they couldn't resist the temptation of the wealth he was offering in exchange for their peasants.

Nobody knew how or why it had started, but suddenly the rumour began to be heard on the whole estate, everyone began to speak about the man in the calash, thought he would soon come, that he had already reached the neighbouring province. Some peasants on nearby estates had heard as much from peasants on other neighbouring estates who also hoped that one day the calash would appear on the roads that crossed the province, a black calash with gilded crests, four handsome black steeds, and riders acting as escorts. One had told another that they had seen him . . . Nobody knew when he would arrive, along which road, whether he would have any roubles left in his purse when he drove on to the master's land, but of course he would, he was so rich he would buy them all and set them free. An edict ruled that serfs could only buy their freedom the day before they died, that until that day arrived, they couldn't buy their right to live as free men despite all the energy they had expended working for their master.

The rumour spread quickly, and there was even the occasional revolt. Peasants and serfs had this one hope, and consequently when the grief and disappointment at not being saved had passed, when nobody had mentioned it for many a month, the story began to re-appear, in whisper after whisper. Why was unclear, perhaps because on another estate everyone was less despondent and, as they trans-ported straw or looked for grain, as they talked among themselves, the serfs would cheer up and say they had seen the man in the calash, the Saviour. And the toil was never-ending, men kept impregnating their wives, and women gave birth to children who would bury them, the landscape couldn't be more desolate, they were always on the watch in case the Saviour's calash appeared from beyond the marshes, rivers and other huge estates that seemed to keep them further from that empti-ness, where you had the feeling that there was nothing anywhere, a scrap of land in the back of beyond, remnants of forest and cultivated land, oppressive in summer and foggy in winter, the repetition of the same situation you saw in so many other places in the country, the repetition of days spent hoping for change, though nothing ever did.

THE TWINS

This is the story the elders tell:

Once upon a long time ago, all this land you see before you was a vast barren waste. A married peasant couple were the only inhabitants in the whole area and they lived by cultivating the land they had been able to irrigate and clear around their hut.

They had been thrown out of the city, the capital of a very prosperous region situated upriver. The city was a wonderful, ancient city, its streets of cobbled stone polished by passing carts and people and always washed clean by rain and snow. The timber and stone houses shone a more brilliant white every morning; each house was the pride and joy of its family. "I am from the house ..." peasants and merchants would say to identify each other and everyone had to respond by saying what their house was like.

With every full moon, a great market was organised in the central square to which merchants came from every town in the region. The stalls surrounded the church that towered above the centre of the square as if it were a jewel cut from white stone. The great gilded dome that graced the belfry could be seen shining from many, many *versts* around and was the point of reference for merchants, pilgrims and travellers. It was a lighthouse in the midst of that ocean of earth.

The river crossed the middle of the city and seemed to be but an excuse to build those magnificent bridges and jetties that were reflected in its calm waters, and the glare from the city's white walls was broken only by four caulked wood doors riveted with iron and bronze.

Far from that city, the man and woman who cultivated those fields struggled to harvest the corn that grew in the earth that they had been able to reclaim from the marshes and creeks. Pavel strapped on the harness and pulled the plough and Galina strove hard to drive the ploughshare deep down. The days were very long and there was no rest for Pavel and Galina, only a hut they had had to build from branches and brushwood with their bare hands.

Those hands had felt such poverty . . .

When they banished them, they didn't let them take anything, they even wondered whether they should allow them to walk off clothed. "Let them feel the cold, if they want to act like wild animals, and not abide by our laws. Let them feel the cold like wild animals" people bawled from the top of the walls, and they received no help from their closest family, from brothers and sisters or parents, nobody stepped forward to defend them, they had committed the worst of crimes, they had disobeyed the governor, they had refused to pay the tithe in order to live in the city.

If a man wanted to marry, he had to accept the city's three laws.

When they reached that point, the elders looked into the eyes of the young: the time had come for their listeners to decide what they would do, faced by the three laws of the city.

*

The first law they must accept was the law of vassalage. The second required you to give over your house to the governor, who immediately ceded it to the vassal in usufruct. The third was the right to the first blood of the bride. It was the price to pay to live in such a beautiful city. All the streets shone the day that Pavel and Galina were sentenced to banishment, to live outside the city.

What a beautiful day! The water of the river seemed calmer and more transparent, the perch more plentiful. From a distance the church seemed taller than ever and the tiles on the house roofs sparkled like the facets of precious stones. Nobody came to bid them farewell, the citizenry insisted everyone should experience the shame of losing their home and their freedom and giving their wife over to the governor, the insult of losing their work, their honour and that of their family. Everyone should be equal, in the city.

Galina and Pavel walked for days before they settled down on the banks of a stream that was formed by the thaw, and after years of shortages and disasters, they finally managed to build one of the biggest *izbas* in the whole district. They had established themselves on land that was free of vassalage, and consequently they themselves had to defend their harvests, the hands that took up spades and hoes had to take up swords and spears with equal determination, the story of mankind. The fruit from their trees and the harvests from their fields increased by the year. They were too far from the city to go there to fetch any provisions, and the merchants found neither hindrances nor obstacles when it came to turning off the main path and going to their izba to buy and to sell.

One day, Galina became pregnant and after nine months of a heavy pregnancy, she gave birth to twins. They called the first Ivan and the second Alexei. Pavel baptised them in the same stream that he used to water his vegetables. They had broad wrists and jutting chins, signs of strength and tenacity, and as both Ivan and Alexei grew, the boundaries of the land their parents cultivated expanded in step with them. All four sowed and reaped the wheat and all four chased off the intruders and thieves that wanted to steal their harvest.

Ivan and Alexei lived for each other. They worked from dawn to dusk, and when it wasn't the season to sow or reap, they hunted. Pavel had taught them well, they hunted enough meat to feed a whole village. And, needless to say, the skills they displayed when hunting they also used to chase off thieves and bandits.

Time passed peacefully in Galina and Pavel's house, but the day came when the twins wanted to leave the nest. They wanted to marry and build homes and have land next to the land they had tilled since childhood. After speaking to Pavel, Galina consulted the merchants who came to the bench on the riverbank and they soon brought two girls, Frida and Tamara. The girls reached an accord with the boys, and the families an agreement in the matter of dowries and capital. The wedding day was set and afterwards a great banquet was held.

However, before they could finish the meal, a messenger came from the governor of the city. The governor demanded ownership of the houses built on the banks of the river, that

Alexei and Ivan should be his vassals and he should have the right to the first blood of both brides. If they refused the governor's demands, they would be thrown off their land, those were the orders from the city.

As soon as the messengers returned to the city, the governor's guard sent out horsemen and archers, and as soon as they reached the fields of Pavel and Galina, the archers set light to the tips of their arrows and burned the crops and the house. Pavel, Galina and Tamara were unable to reach the river, and the twins and Frida had to bury them under the ashes of their house, mud to mud, ashes to ashes.

Perhaps some felt sad when they heard this part of the story, but then the old folk waved their hands, as if to tell them to wait, to save their sadness for later. And then continued:

Ivan and Alexei wept over their dead, fasted, and, after a week, went hunting and began to rebuild a house on the spot where old Pavel had built his. Then, of course, the history of mankind repeated itself. Men are always giving things to one another, sometimes words, sometimes love, sometimes presents and sometimes revenge.

The day when they had the biggest fair in the city, the market that the most people attended, Alexei slipped inside its walls. Everyone was happy, musicians played in streets, in squares, in houses, on balconies and in galleries. Partying, more partying in streets in the centre and at balls held in the governor's palace. Carousing, singing and drinking. Until darkness fell, and the city sentinels shut the city gates.

From afar the city looked like a crown studded with precious stones. The fire burned houses and palaces and the walls simply shot the flames into the air, as if the city were burning on top of an incense burner. By night, the glow was like a blood-red moon's, sparks were more numerous than stars . . . Alexei died inside the city, burned in the fire, like the torch that is consumed in the heart of a huge bonfire. Only a few families survived, those who lived by the river and could find a boat.

After two days of fire, the city still gleamed like a ruby by night, a huge brazier of red-hot stone, gone were the church, palaces and houses, and the streets were blocked by the walls that had collapsed.

That is the story the elders tell when the youngest ask why their house must be the price they must pay to live in the city, why they have to swear to be vassals, why they have to let the soldiers snatch their wives and take them to the governor Ivan. That is what the elders reply, staring at the ground, when the youngest complain of the cruel ways of the descendants of that Ivan who married the beautiful Frida so long ago. The city is his because the great-grandfather of his great-grandfather rebuilt it from the ashes of the city that had banished his family.

SERGEI ALEKSANDR'S LAST SUPPER

It is hard to describe the ravages wrought by an epidemic to those who have never endured one.

As for me, unfortunately, I have seen all kinds in my long life. I have travelled the world and seen scourges everywhere. On my journeys across Africa I have witnessed how diarrhoea decimated the peoples most hidden and protected from the presence of the white man. I have boarded vessels where scurvy, like a huge ghost, cast into the ocean's waves the bodies of sailors, and I have come to the Americas where the breath of a single feverish pig was enough to kill thousands of Indians not accustomed to such a disease. I am no stranger to leprosy. I have journeyed for days in regions it has devastated, I have seen dysentery, Malta fever, I have seen villages abandoned because of smallpox and hospitals packed with men disfigured by measles or mumps, but if you want the truth from me I must say I have never seen such horrendous suffering or so many defy death so stubbornly as during my stay in Pryvolchevo.

Pryvolchevo was the last stop on a journey that led me to visit the whole of Russia. I like Russia, it is a unique, extraordinary land; one could almost say after exploring it that Russia is the earth. Forgive me if I ramble. I was telling you how I had come to Pryvolchevo. At the time, I had just travelled across the land of the Tartars and the Cossacks. During my six-month stay in iron-ore and coalfields, in work camps for the new seams in Siberia, influenza and pneumonia were our daily bread. I continued my Russian wanderings until I arrived in Boldino, the administrative capital for Pryvolchevo.

As soon as I reached Boldino and could talk to my host, I realised I would find it difficult to continue on my way. Many cities between Boldino and Moscow had been declared closed by the plague, and although there were hidden paths that skirted their walls and the smallest villages too, the army had established checkpoints to prevent the population moving. It was a pretty city and I suppose that long afterwards it was pretty once again. I have never returned, perhaps one of my rider companions has, or perhaps not.

I immediately befriended officers, local mayors and governors, and they all wanted to hear stories of my travels. One individual stood out among the influential people in the town: a curly-haired, bright-eyed young man who was there, as was common knowledge, because he had enraged the Tsar with his satirical poems. Sergei Aleksandr was his name, a young man who inspired enthusiasm in all who listened to him: he became very popular because of his hunting parties, soirées and recitals, political harangues that the local rulers turned a blind eye to. After making my first introductions, I often paid him a visit, the soldiers had blocked all roads out of Boldino and I had time on my hands. Besides, my adventures and deeds simultaneously amused, interested, saddened and angered him.

Days went by and nothing happened. Long, long evenings, arguments about France and the Tsar, windy days, sunny days and snowswept days followed by windy days and sunny days and run-of-the-mill days, until one afternoon one of the lackeys of the house rushed into the sitting room where we were arguing about Russia, as we always did.

"Master, master," said the lackey, "they have declared an outbreak of plague and closed the city gates. There have been three cases in five days, master."

That same night, after collecting up money and belongings, Sergei Aleksandr managed to bribe a couple of guards and led us along hidden paths to the village of Pryvolchevo, a small village of one hundred and fifty souls a few *versts* from Boldino, that had never had any cases of the plague. We rented a house, and, to fight off loneliness, we organised a supper every night to which the peasants generously contributed food and drink. It was their way of exorcising the fear aroused by the proximity of the plague: dancing, the recitation of long poems the youngest had been taught by their grandparents, and vodka. By the end of the week time dragged yet again and nothing surprising; conversations about Russia, Russia and more Russia, and snow and sun. Until, finally, people began to die from cholera in Pryvolchevo; first the elderly and children and then men and women of every age and from every social class.

Nonetheless, there was a big party almost every other day, we even concluded that one day should be reserved for burials and for the necessary respects mourning imposes and the rest to celebrate the fact the plague had still not felled any of those present. Sergei Aleksandr had showed a special interest in holding those parties. Right from the start, when we arrived in the village, he began to tell stories to the children in the house next door. Gradually, the children from the whole neighbourhood came to hear him, and what was a way of entertaining children and distracting them from the general gloom and unease was soon transformed into an occasion for the whole village. So much so that we had to change our meeting place and move to a stockade. Everybody was keen to go to Godunov's stockade. Sergei Aleksandr told them stories of ancient heroes riding across the steppes; sometimes, and I saw this with my own eyes, he got up from his chair, climbed on the table and shouted even louder, and acted as if he were mounting his steed and fighting against the Tartars. The eyes of children and old folk alike bulged from their sockets, and they waved their legs and stamped their feet when Sergei Aleksandr spurred on his horse-chair, its back against his chest, and everyone held their breath watching that chair penetrate the serried ranks of Tartars. Every night, when his mouth was parched, the peasants brought a bottle of vodka and raised a toast to exorcise fear, in the end someone always dared to raise his voice and his glass against the plague, as they would raise them against winter in dances in March.

None of the inhabitants of Pryvolchevo had ever experienced a situation like that. The peasants living in the most distant *izbas* were frightened by the plague. When they heard about the first cases, they rarely came to barter skins or sell partridges and hares. Their absence, however, was short-lived, because, although they were afraid of the plague, the noise from the dance we held every night in the stockade attracted them as wild animals are drawn to the hand that may conceal danger. They were and they weren't, I remember them well, approaching along the road with burning torches and stopping every other second to make up their minds yet again whether to enter the village or return home. Finally, one harangued against fear and they all entered Godunov's stockade.

By day, the men hunted in the forest and the women washed clothes and ensured that those stricken by the plague had what they needed. We decided to place all the sick people in a barn a long way from the village. Every day a newly stricken villager entered the barn, someone suffering the first symptoms who took responsibility for looking after those who were in the last throes. The villagers left food, wood and basins of boiling water by the door in case anyone felt like washing clothes. The healthy only entered the plague barn to take out the dead and bury them. When someone died, the sick hung a black cloth from one of the windows and the villagers went to fetch the body. As the priest had fled, and as the one telling you this now and Sergei Aleksandr were the only ones who knew how to read, we read the verses about the resurrection of Lazarus, and the villagers went home, their spirits lifted, the resurrection of the flesh, O Sergei Aleksandr, how passionately you raised your hands to heaven and asked for that soul to be admitted . . .

By night, storytelling was the only way to make those men and women forget their fear: "Sergei Aleksandr, tell us what happened, when you rode through that blizzard." And he then recited a poem by Zhukovsky – *The horses bounded over snow drifts, across hills and plains* – and immediately launched into the story about Mr Gavrila Gavrilovitch and her daughter Maria . . .

"Sergei Aleksandr, tell us what vast Siberia is like," they asked, and Sergei Aleksandr took a lump of coal and drew a map on the timber floor and told them what was to be found in every corner of Great Mother Siberia.

"There are bears here, seals there and further on Lapps and on the other side Mongols and Tartars . . . You should see the houses of ice where the Lapps live . . ."

As the days passed, the number of stricken increased, and now there wasn't a burial every now and then, but three or four bodies at a time. Moreover, the news from outside couldn't be worse, nearby cities had been closed and they had declared the whole region to be in quarantine.

The population of Pryvolchevo was rapidly diminishing, and there was more and more to eat for supper. At the beginning there were a hundred of us bringing the victuals and vodka we had stored to the feast. And though what I am about to relate brings little but shame upon us, we broke down the doors of the houses of families that would eat no more from their pantries. We had had more salted meat and flour than we could eat, and more and more people were entering (and leaving, may they rest in peace) the plague-stricken barn, so we had no fear of ever going hungry.

The villagers' character was changing. The other villages in the area had always described the inhabitants of Pryvolchevo as extremely pious, distinguished and thrifty, people who liked order and cleanliness and knew how to comport themselves. The heirs and daughters of Pryvolchevo were renowned for being honest, industrious folk you could rely on. However, from the time that the first cases of the plague were declared, they had begun to act in a more daring, less restrained way. On the one hand, the plague terrified them and made them more timid. The values with which they had been brought up, lack of excess, the golden mean, were eroding because their main objective was gone, the ideals that had been inculcated now meant nothing: why respect Father if Father was no more? Why be honest to protect the good name of the family, if the family was no more? They had been taught not to steal, and now broke into every house looking for food; the priest had taught them prayers, but was no longer there to chant . . . They were no longer the hardworking, thrifty folk of Pryvolchevo. Besides, on the other hand, that man, Sergei Aleksandr had come to the village with me, a man who liked long nights and journeying throughout Russia, the man who said he had met the Tsar, and was asked to raise their spirits every evening to the point that it seemed possible to forget the plague and the deaths of close relatives, of fathers, sons or wives.

The long evenings were also changing. At the beginning, as I said earlier, the men and women came simply to listen to Sergei Aleksandr, to hear him tell of his adventures, whether real or imagined. As I also told you, these tales always ended with a toast, but lo and behold, the gathering started to be held earlier and earlier as if the people in the village were more afraid of being alone than of any chance they might catch the disease by rubbing shoulders with others. No doubt the plague advanced so swiftly because we survivors continued to meet nightly and act rashly against the often repeated advice of doctors of the time, isolation of the sick and isolation of the healthy. Even so, many swore we had been lucky to enjoy the presence of Sergei Aleksandr, and that, without him, those weeks would indeed have been unbearable.

I don't know if it was because we were afraid of returning to our gloomy homes after listening to Sergei Aleksandr or couldn't face going out into the blizzards when we were so warm and cosy inside the stockade, but the truth is that after that first supper, those feasts weren't only a meeting-place for all those of us who were still breathing, but also a place where we stayed on to sleep. And if right at the start those suppers were traditionally frugal, the women kept putting more and more meat into the pot, and during supper the transparency of water gave way to the clarity of vodka. The gargantuan feasts were followed by the now much appreciated stories told by Sergei Aleksandr, and the poetry he improvised, standing on the table, line after line, to the applause of both men and women.

We gathered earlier and earlier and went to sleep later and later. We drank more by the day and the villagers became more daring in what they said and did. All those who were still alive came to these suppers, and their children as well, who played in the barn at the top of the stockade. Everybody came, widowers and orphaned children, mothers bereft of children and sisters-in-law who had lost their sisters but not their brothers-in-law. The plague had killed the oldest and feeblest and the numbers supping grew fewer and fewer. The women took care to remove the chairs, nobody wanted to see empty chairs that undermined the morale of the healthy and reminded them of those who had once sat there. Everything possible was done to make us survivors as comfortable as possible. After supping and listening to the ever more stunning stories told by Sergei Aleksandr, a fiddler played traditional tunes and the women sang in chorus, and later, the fiddler struck up a polka and everyone took to the floor. And naturally, the men who had lost their wives and the wives who had lost their husbands danced together as did sisters-in-law with brothers-in-law, and the youngster who had always desired the maiden who had died now danced with her sister, and the laughter got louder, and the wit and jokes and sweet words they shared were so welcome, that if at first shame and blushes (oh dear, Dame Morality) prevented them from making the final move, in the depths of night, each couple sought out a hidden corner of the stockade. The children slept, and each night what began as a feast ended in an orgy. One woman bared a breast as she danced and another lifted her skirt, and the men added to the fun with obscene gestures. The glee brought by vodka did the rest, and I can tell you I have seen men and women rolling over the stockade floor and under the tables as couples chased each other, and I have seen love made to the sound of clapping hands, and all because those men and those women were afraid that each night would be their last, and wanted to frighten off the plague that threatened them.

Ay, I saw how the men of Pryvolchevo drank endlessly, and how the women went after them to make love, and how they all slept together, side by side. In the end, they only left the stockade to do what nature forces men and women to do, and to get clothes, food and water and return to the stockade. There was always someone who was not allowed to stay one more night, those whose bellies were beginning to mess up, who were outlawed and banished to the plague-ridden barn.

Every day there were fewer of the hundred or so of us who began feasting in the stockade, soon only a dozen remained. The peasants still insisted that Sergei Aleksandr told his stories, but Sergei Aleksandr who had crossed the whole of Siberia, who had travelled through the Mongolian deserts, who had sailed the largest, fastest flowing rivers of

Russia, no longer told of his adventures, he improvised a song that got longer by the day, a song against the plague, a song that mocked the plague, that mocked the dead, that mocked the living and mocked the fate that had befallen them all and he sang of the days in the stockade as the happiest they had ever lived, O Sergei Aleksandr, the bard who liked to climb on the table and tell us to have no fear of death and to mock the plague and raise your glass to toast it . . . I must thank you for all those toasts! I must thank you, last survivors of Pryvolchevo that I finally abandoned, thank you for your good cheer and daring. Thank you for the many toasts you drank to my health, peasants of Pryvolchevo.

Oh, what times were had in the stockade, I have never seen so much happiness and so much suffering, times of terrible fear, of music and women, of vodka and dancing, despairing happiness, though happiness all the same. And what a pity that one fine day, you too, Sergei Aleksandr, were stricken by the plague, but you knew death comes to all men, is the great leveller, you knew that my companion makes no distinctions between rich and poor, between wits and fools . . . That was your last night, that pitch-black night when you looked me in the eyes and sang the hymn to the plague you had been composing for so long, the hymn you sang during those last suppers, a hymn in my honour, my hymn. Did you recognise me?

I left Pryvolchevo the next day, Sergei Aleksandr. You wanted a different death, years later, but you chose an end that didn't sully the nobility that always accompanied you: a bullet, a duel you fought with yourself. I departed Pryvolchevo the very next day.

FRANCESC SERÉS is a Catalan writer, born in Saidí, Aragon in 1972. He studied Fine Arts and Anthropology at the Universitat de Barcelona and now works as a professor of art history. His novels, short stories and plays have been translated into Spanish and other European languages. He won Catalonia's National Literature Prize for the trilogy of novels collected in *Manures and Marbles* (2003) and both the City of Barcelona Prize and the Critics' Prize for *Russian Stories*.

PETER BUSH now works as a freelance translator in Barcelona after a five-year stint as Director of the British Centre for Literary Translation and Professor of Literary Translation at the University of East Anglia. He was awarded the 2012 Ramón del Valle-Inclán Prize for his translation of *Exiled From Almost Everywhere* by Juan Goytisolo.